# iBT 新托福閱讀

## 解構式 學習

化繁為「剪」

王盟雄 ◎著

U0057212

# Score High on iBT Reading Test!

# 最新具指標性的iBT新托福閱讀書

只需要會【剪】下閱讀文章中的枝微末節＋【密集演練】iBT新托福閱讀考試
必碰上的自然、地理、歷史、科學等10大學術類型題目,同時吸收重點文法、
一窺化「繁」為「簡」的密技,縮短應考時間,輕鬆應戰 iBT 新托福閱讀!

◎ 最詳實擬真!
　iBT新托福閱讀文章、考題演練與深度分析:
　→ 閱讀能力＋字彙量 同步快速提升
　　突破iBT 110+ !

# Author's & Editor's Words
## 作者序／編者序

## 作者序

　　坊間英文書籍汗牛充棟，乍看之下似乎應有盡有。事實上，只要定眼一瞧，就能發現有關 TOEFL 閱讀的書籍少得可憐，說是屈指可數也不為過。按理說，凡是出國留學，大多都難逃 TOEFL 的洗禮，怎麼相關書籍會寥寥無幾？從 2006 年起，台灣 TOEFL 改成 iBT 形式，也就是 Internet-Based Test 網路化測驗，完全透過電腦與耳機來作答，揚棄傳統紙筆介面。除非透過電腦實作，否則單靠紙本介面很難如實呈現出來，這可能是出版商對 TOEFL 閱讀題材提不起興趣的原因之一。因為跟我們從小到大所熟悉的紙筆測驗迥異，因此在這裡鼓勵初次報名 TOEFL 的讀者最至少要體驗一下 The TOEFL iBT® Interactive Sampler。這是 ETS®（Educational Testing Service 美國教育測驗服務社）為了方便 TOEFL 考生熟悉 iBT 操作介面所製作的免費小軟體，裡面有一套完整聽說讀寫的模擬試題，下載連結如下：

　　https://www.ets.org/Media/Tests/TOEFL/exe/TOEFL_Sampler_2014.exe

　　假如口袋夠深，還可以購買 TPO（TOEFL® Practice Online）「托福線上全真模擬測驗」，一次美金 $ 45.95 元。這不只是 ETS® 官方最權威的 TOEFL 線上模擬考，練習完以後電腦還能馬上告知得分。網址如下：https://toeflpractice.ets.org/

　　TOEFL 閱讀之道無它，惟辭彙與長難句而已矣！職是之故，提升閱

讀能力最核心的要項有兩點：一，閱讀基礎能力和實力的提升；二，熟諳 iBT 閱讀出題思路、出題點以及解題原則。要想提升基礎能力，除了每天單字都要有固定進帳之外，做練習、分析長難句也不可少。不只做錯的題目必須訂正，還要深入揣摩、理解每道題背後的考點何在？因為

iBT 閱讀的答案 100% 出自原文，不管哪一題都對應到原文中的某一句話。既然答案是針對那句話重新改寫詮釋，所以絕對不能倚賴自己直覺的記憶或判斷直接望文生義，而是要原文定位，切切實實的找到 ETS® 命題者鎖定的那句話，然後看看哪個選項是那句話的精確同義改寫，否則很容易掉進 ETS® 挖好的陷阱裡。雖然答案經過精心變形後顯得朦朦朧朧，但是錯誤選項卻十分有規律性，例如倒果為因、顛倒是非、以假亂真、張冠李戴、無中生有。簡而言之，就是仔細推敲答案的微言大義和圈出考點，亦即分析錯誤選項錯在哪個地方以及正確選項會具備那些特點、特徵。本書目的就是幫助讀者培養出這種實力！

王盟雄

## 編者序

　　全書收錄 iBT 新托福閱讀考試必碰得到的自然、地理、商學、行銷、文化、藝術、歷史、科學等 10 大學術類型，教讀者以文法的角度，如連接詞、關係子句等，拆解閱讀長句，直接看到問題的答案，縮短閱讀考試猶豫的作答時間，同時提升答題正確率！

編輯部敬上

# *Instructions* 使用說明

**1, 2**
收錄最常考的題目搭配長難句最常用的句型文法。哪個領域、文法不熟，就從哪個章節下手，迅速解決問題！

**3**
貼心的書側索引，呼應文章主題，方便查找，也加深學習印象！

**4**
收錄仿照 TOEFL 命題格式的短文，一短文分為 (1)、(2) 兩篇，有助讀者快速熟悉考試模式！

**5**
每篇短文的重要單字皆粗體、套色，便於對照、掌握全文脈絡，不遺漏任何細節！

---

*Unit 2-8* | The Ultimate Delivery System (2) 終極快遞系統 (2)

**The Ultimate Delivery System (2)**
**終極快遞系統（2）**

**Unit 2-8**

閱讀原文：試用 3 分鐘的時間念完文章，記得先把中文遮上，並翻頁看題目問什麼。計時開始！

**The Ultimate Delivery System (2)**

Take the case of Mr. Rahman, an office worker, for example. His dabba has a black swastika, a yellow dot, and a red slash. Elsewhere there is a white cross in a black circle. The first symbols tell the dabbawalas the train station to go to, the line to take, and where to get off; the remaining ones indicate the district and the building and floor where they need to be delivered. At 10 a.m. the first dabbawala turns up to collect Mr. Rahman's dabba from his wife at home. The dabba sets off on its journey. By 12:30 Mr. Rahman is tucking into his lunch.

It is a hazardous occupation riding a bicycle with a huge tray of dabbas, or rushing across busy roads to get to an office building on the other side. During the monsoon season, dabbawalas have to wade through water to get to their customers. If a dabbawala is incapacitated, another one will take over the dabba delivery lest the dabbas should fail to arrive at their destination in time.

**終極快遞系統（2）**

就拿一位白領上班族拉曼先生為例。他的 dabba 上面有一個黑色卐字、一個黃色圓點、一條紅色斜線；其他地方還有一個白色十字、黑色圓圈。第一組符號告訴 dabbawala 去哪個火車站、哪裡搭車、哪裡下車；其餘那一組則指示要送到哪一區、哪一棟大樓的某幾樓。早上十點第一個 dabbawala 在拉曼先生家門口出現，從他老婆手中取得 dabba，這便當就展開它的行程。到 12:30 時，拉曼先生正埋首吃午餐了。

這行業要拿著裝有 dabba 的大托盤騎單車，或者是匆忙穿梭的街道到另一邊的辦公大樓，真是險象環生。在雨季期間，dabbawala 還必須涉水去找客戶。如果 dabbawala 失能，另一名會接手，以免那個便當不能及時送達目的地。

104     105

## 6, 7, 8

仿照 TOEFL 閱讀題必碰上的三種不同題型，分別為 1. 置入題、 2. 主旨題，與 3. 劃底線的基本訊息題，全方位強化讀者的解題能力，獲取高分！

### 考題演練及解析

Look at the four letters that indicate where the following sentence could be added to the passage.

**It will not be long before wholesalers buy these flowers and then re-export them to other markets across the globe.**

Where could the sentence best fit?

看看文章裡四個字母，哪個地方可以把下面句子安插進去
不久批發商會買下這些花，然後再將它們出口到世界其他市場。
這句子放哪裡最合適？

### 解析

答案 | (C)

❶ 一般來說，假如插入題型的題
代名詞或 this、those、here
天上掉下來的禮物！因為只要
詞的本尊揪出來，拼湊出邏輯

❷ 不過看不看到這一題一開頭就
個 It 是代表時間，就好比
前後文之中哪一個名詞。

70

### 考題演練及解析

**Which of the following statements about the dabbawala is supported by this passage?**
(A) The dabbawalas begin to work early in the morning.
(B) The dabbawalas must learn to recognize a unique but complicated abstract symbols so as to deliver each dabba to the right customer wherever in Mumbai the person is.
(C) After lunch, the dabbawalas collect the dabba from desks they delivered to, and bring them back to home where it started from.
(D) Should a dabbawala have an accident, his coworker cover his shift to ensure the dabba won't miss deadline.

根據本文，以下關於 dabbawala 的陳述何者為真？
(A) dabbawala 一大早就開始工作
(B) dabbawala 必須學習辨識一套獨特卻複雜的抽象符號
便把便當正確無誤地送到客人手上，不管那人在孟買哪
方
(C) 午餐後，dabbawala 去客戶辦公室取回便當，然後把
帶回客戶家裡，亦即原先最早的起點
(D) 萬一 dabbawala 發生意外，他的同事會代他的班，確保

106

### 考題演練及解析

**Which of the following best expresses the essential information in the underlined sentence? Incorrect answer choices change the meaning in important ways or leave out essential information.**
(A) Though popular and widespread in other countries, the word game appealed to a very small group of people in America.
(B) Despite its popularity worldwide, the crossword puzzle was illegal in America.
(C) The crossword puzzle won massive popularity.
(D) Most crossword puzzles were so hard that very few people could work them out.

以下哪一句最能表達出劃底線句子的基本訊息？不正確的答案選項會以重要方式改變句意，或者遺漏基本訊息
(A) 雖然這個文字遊戲在其他國家大受歡迎而且十分普及，但是在美國只吸引一小撮人。
(B) 雖然填字遊戲全球火手可熱，但是在美國卻是違法的。
(C) 填字遊戲人氣妙得強強滾。
(D) 大部分填字遊戲非常難，極少人解得出來。

148

# *Instructions* 使用說明

**9**

每單元於考題後，立即有詳細的重點文法解析，抽絲剝繭了解文法、理解文章，其中還有單字的字源、字根補充，大大提升閱讀理解力！

**10**

條列式解析以活潑的口吻呈現，透過一一詳述每個選項的細節，破解艱澀的難題，有助讀者循序漸進累積閱讀實力！

---

*Unit 2-5 |* Hunch or Reason? (1) 直覺或理性（1）

 **解析**

答案 | (C)

❶ 這一題核心就在 the jury is still out。jury 是「陪審團」，按照英美國家的審判程序，被告是否有非由陪審團裁定。庭審結束後，陪審員離席，進入陪審室討論被告是否有罪以及如何定罪。在陪審員沒有回到法庭之前，審判結果無從得知。例如：The jury is still out on whether the jerrybuilt houses will be torn down.（那些偷工減料的房子是否要拆除目前還是一個大問號。）。得悉背後的典故，答案昭然若揭即 (C)。就算不知道這典故，後面的 or 還是洩漏了天機，因為 or 本身就暗示著不確定，這意味這雖像真假難辨。

❷ (C) 選項的 **genuine** 跟 **gene**「基因」同源。如果具有某種 gene，就意味這是與生俱來，不是人為假冒，當然是「真實的」。同理，所謂 **genius**「天才」就意味天才能是天生，並非後天栽培的 **ingenuous** 字形、字義跟 genuine 比較像，意思是「天真的、坦率的」；**ingenious** 字形、字義跟 genius 比較像，意思是「聰明的、精巧的」。兩個字的字首 in-都是 in 的意思，也就是 in the genes 來自基因的遺傳。

89

---

*Unit 2-8 |* The Ultimate Delivery System (2) 終極快遞系統（2）

個便當不至於錯過時限。

**解析**

答案 | (D)

❶ 早上十點 dabbawala 才開始去客戶家裡拿便當，工作時間應該是 late in the morning，所以 (A) 不對。

❷ (B) 幾乎都正確，但是卻出現一顆老鼠屎，以至於整碗粥全報銷了：complicated。從本文第二句話就知道便當前前後後就五個符號。十點時 the first dabbawala 來拿便當，注意那個 first，這意味只是便當快遞接力中的第一棒而已，中間還要轉好幾手，每一位 dabba 接棒後只要會辨識專屬自己負責那一個符號就行了，這樣還不夠簡單嗎？幹這一行的大多數是文盲，假如這套編碼符號系統太複雜，豈不是三不五時就搞得天下大亂。因此這套系統 abstract「抽象」沒錯，但是並不 complicated「複雜」。

❸ 注意要看清題目。(C) 選項敘述可能沒錯，但是本文並沒有提到這件事，因此 (C) 還是不對。

❹ 注意 (D) 是假設法的倒裝句型，順來應該是 If a dabbawala should have an accident…，會用 should 意味發生機率不高。這選項正好反映出文章的最後一句，所以答案就是 (D)。

107

11

---

⚙ **深度應用分析：對付閱讀就是要化「繁」為「簡」，先刪去( )、[] 內的文字，找出主要的主詞和動詞！**

❶ If (a dabbawala is incapacitated), [(another one will take over the dabba delivery) lest (the dabba should fail to arrive at their destination in time)].

**解析**

❶ 這句話有兩個連接詞 if 和 lest，lest 後面引導的子句常常會加上 should。這個 should 也可以省略，不過省略歸省略，後面的動詞還是要原形。例如：He brought an umbrella with him lest it (should) rain this afternoon.（他帶了傘，以免今天下午下雨。）

❷ lest = in case = for fear that，所以後面那句也可以寫成：… another one will take over the dabba delivery in case the dabbas fails to arrive at their destination in time.

❸ incapacitate = in(not) + capacit + ate(動詞字尾)
incapacitate 這個字雖然有點深度，但是從字形依然看得出來跟 capacity 很像。萬一很不幸還是不知道 capacity 是何方神聖，那麼應該認識它的形容詞 capable 了吧？是的，be

108

---

*Unit 2-8 | The Ultimate Delivery System (2) 終極快遞系統（2）*

capable of 曝光率高多了，知名度雖然還比不上 be able to，但是也算是小有名氣；

| 形容詞 | capable | 「能幹的、有能力的」 |
| 名詞 | capacity | 「才能、能力」 |
| 動詞 | capacitate | 「使有能力」 |

capacitate 加上表否定的字首 in-，incapacitate 當然是「失去能力」。

❷ The first symbols tell the Dabbawalas (the train station to go to), (the line to take), and (where to get off); the remaining ones indicate [the district and the building and floor (where they need to be delivered)].

**解析**

❶ 這句話以分號連接兩句，各自說明便當上兩組符號代表什麼意思。The first symbols 是指前面提到的 a black swastika、a yellow dot、a red slash 這些符號；remaining 後面的 ones 代替前面的 symbols，也就是 a white cross、black circle 這些符號。

❷ 之所以會需要這一套符號系統，無非是便當快遞業者很多都是 illiterate「文盲」。要讓所有文盲都看得懂，這套符號系統當然必須要簡單明瞭。

ch 1
ch 2
ch 3
ch 4
ch 5
ch 6

---

✎ **11**

看每單元精選長難句，跟著本書做拆解、化「繁」為「剪／減」，理出頭緒，把句子重點馬上抓出來！

# References
## 參考書目及網站

Encyclopædia Britannica, Inc. *Encyclopaedia Britannica Ultimate Edition*, London: Encyclopædia Britannica (UK) Ltd, 2014. DVD.

Microsoft Corporation. *Microsoft Student with Encarta Premium 2009*. Washington: Microsoft Inc., 2009. DVD.

Funk, Wilfred. *Word Origins and Their Romantic Stories*. New York: Random House Value Publishing, 1978. Print.

Ayto, John. *Dictionary of Word Origins*. New York: Arcade Publishing, Inc., 1993. Print.

Fowler, H. W. *A Dictionary ofModern English Usage*. New York: Oxford University Press, 1985. Print.

A. S. Hornby. Guide to Patterns and Usage in English. New York: Oxford University Press, 1975. Print.

Carter, Ronald, Michael McCarthy, Geraldine Mark, and Anne O'Keeffe. *English Grammar Today*. Cambridge: Cambridge University Press, 2011, Print.

Hammond, Wallie. *Peterson's Master TOEFL Reading Skills*. Lawrenceville: Peterson's A Netnet Company, 2007. Print.

Hearn,William Edward. *The TOEFL Master's Guide to a Perfect Score*. Estero: PraxisGroup International Language AKADEMEIA, 2015. Kindle.

旋元佑（1998）。《旋元佑文法》。新北：經典傳訊文化。

陳啟賢、陳明亮（2008）。《活用圖解英文法》。台北：建弘出版社。

葉珍珍、Sunny Chiu（2010）。《圖表解構英文文法》。台北：希伯崙公司。

空中美語叢書編輯群(2008)。《文法總動員》。台北：空中美語。

蔣平（1992）。《全真托福文法結構精華》。台北：先見出版公司

陳奕（2015）。2015-2017 陳奕 iBT 托福閱讀。台北：哈佛英語出版社。

李傳偉（2008）。新托福閱讀高分策略。北京：高等教育出版社。

徐西坤、王鑫（2012）。新說文解字細說英語詞根詞源。北京：中國水利水電出版社

https://zh.wikipedia.org/w/index.php?title=%E9%A6%96%E9%A1%B5&variant=zh-tw

http://www.newworldencyclopedia.org/entry/Info:Main_Page

http://www.biography.com/

http://www.etymonline.com/

http://www.bartleby.com/

http://dictionary.cambridge.org/

http://www.ldoceonline.com/

# Contents 目次

*Chapter* **3** 從拆解文化題目，
看關係子句的角色

*Chapter* **4** 從拆解藝術、人文類題目，
看分詞構句、介系詞的角色

## Chapter 5　從拆解歷史類題目，看看補述用法的角色

*Chapter* **6** 從拆解科學、科技類題目，
看不定詞、動名詞的角色

# World Habitats (1)

# 世界棲息地（1）

 閱讀原文：試用 **3** 分鐘的時間念完文章，記得先把中文遮上，並翻頁看題目問什麼。計時開始！

## World Habitats (1)

With the differences in climate and vegetation, the earth can be divided into separate ecological systems, within each of which there are ecological communities sustaining their own plant and animal habitats. The **barren** region encircling the North Pole is marked by long, cold winters. Nevertheless, it is home to many types of plants and animals. Mosses and grasses exist in the frozen tundra. Moose, ducks, and weasels can also be found there.

Frigid and dry, **Antarctica** at the South Pole is almost **devoid** of plants. The wild animals are thriving, though, thanks to nourishment provided by the sea. Microscopic creatures in sea feed a multitude of tiny floating animals called zooplankton, which also become food source for a variety of birds, fish, and **mammals**.

Even more uninhabitable than the regions at the polar tips of the earth is the desert, because extreme heat and a lack of water make it a **hostile** environment for living organisms. Nevertheless, many plants, such as cacti, and animals, such as camels, lizards, and other reptiles, have managed to survive in these hot, dry conditions.

## 世界棲息地（1）

由於地球上氣候與植被的差異，地球上的不同的生態系統因而有所區分。每個系統內有生態社群，每個生態社群裡還有特有的動植物棲息地。環繞著北極圈這片貧瘠之地最顯明的就是漫長的寒冬，然而這裡卻是許多動植物的所在地。結冰的凍原上長著苔癬和青草，也可以看到麋鹿、野鴨、貂。

位在南極的南極大陸又乾又冷，幾乎寸草不生。儘管如此，幸虧大海提供了食物，這裡的動物不只種類繁多還欣欣向榮。小到不能再小的海洋生物養活了大批大批的浮游動物，這些浮游動物又成為各種鳥類、魚類、哺乳類的食物。

比地球兩極地區更加不適合居住的就是沙漠，因為酷熱缺水

讓這裡成為生物都難以為繼的不利環境。然而還是有像仙人掌之類的植物以及像駱駝、蜥蜴、其他爬蟲類之類的動物在這乾熱條件下苟活倖存。

 ## 考題演練及重點文法解說

**It can be inferred from this passage that**

(A) of all the earth's ecological systems, the desert is the most difficult place to live.

(B) almost all Antarctic animals are herbivores.

(C) nearly every kind of arctic animal feeds on very small animals which drift in the sea.

(D) climate changes may exert differing effects on the same species of plant in different areas with identical climatic conditions.

從這篇文章可以推論出

(A) 所有地球生態系統中，沙漠是最難以生存的地方。

(B) 幾乎所有南極的動物都是草食動物。

(C) 幾乎每一種北極動物都以漂浮在海中的小動物為主食。

(D) 氣候變遷可能對處於相同氣候條件但是不同地區的相同種類植物產生不同的影響。

# 解析

答案│(A)

❶ 從開頭兩段可以得知不管北極還是南極，條件都極為險惡，這關鍵句又指出沙漠比兩極更糟糕，最糟糕的當然是沙漠了，因此答案是 (A)。(D) 選項完全與本文無關，因此先予以排除。從第二段可以得知，南極大陸幾乎沒有任何植物，所有動物不得不以海裡浮游生物為主食，然後大大小小構成食物鏈，應該是 carnivore 肉食動物占大多數才對，但是 (B) 選項卻說是 herbivore 草食動物，正好相反。(C) 選項乍看之下似乎很正確，但是注意選項裡所提到的是 arctic animal 北極動物，北極大半動物並非以浮游動物為主食。

❷ TOEFL 考試碰到推論題型時，不能像一般細節、釋義題型一樣，從上下文中根據同義字、反義字來找出關鍵句，這樣做會讓你大失所望。這並不是說推論題型就沒有關鍵句，而是所謂「推論」就意味答案不會明說。

ch
1

從拆解自然、地理類題目，看連接詞的角色 1

ch
2

ch
3

ch
4

ch
5

ch
6

❶ (With the differences in climate and vegetation),**the earth can be** divided into separate ecological systems, [within each of which there are ecological communities (sustaining their own plant and animal habitats.)]

👉 解析

❶ 這句話重點是位在中間的主要結構：… **the earth can be divided into separate ecological systems**…，透過這部分來導出整篇文章有關生態系統的介紹；其次是句首的介系詞片語 **With the differences in climate and vegetation,** … ，透過這片語來指出劃分生態系統的依據有二，一個是 climate 氣候，一個是 vegetation 植被；至於後面 [ ] 內拉得很長的關係代名詞子句由於沒傳遞多少重要訊息，反倒無足輕重。

❷ 這個句子一看就感覺綱舉目張，具備主題句的架式。TOEFL 文章不像一般書籍雜誌結構鬆散，最大的特徵就是每段開頭第一、二句往往就是主題句。看懂主題句十分重要，因為透過這些句子，很快就能掌握整篇文章的大意。因此一進 TOEFL 電腦系統，不要急著作答，最好先把每段主題句瀏覽一下。

❷ (Even more uninhabitable than the regions at the polar tips of the earth is **the desert**) because (extreme heat and a lack of water make it a hostile environment for living organisms.)

### 解析

❶ 從屬連接詞 **because** 連接兩個句子，重點是前面的倒裝句 **Even more uninhabitable than the regions at the polar tips of the earth is the desert**；至於後面表原因的附屬子句，因為所提的是一般基本常識，只要認識 desert「沙漠」，即使不懂 extreme、hostile 這些單字也無傷大雅。

❷ 前面句子的原本應該是 **The desert is even more uninhabitable than the regions at the polar tips of the earth**。聽取訊息時，我們的注意力常常會集中在最後幾個字，因此寫作時為了讓讀者注意到重要訊息，會故意把要強調的字眼置於句尾，這就是倒裝句的妙用。例如：
Just as surprising was his love for clothes.（同樣令人驚奇的是，他對衣服的喜愛）

從拆解自然、地理類題目，看連接詞的角色 1

# World Habitats (2)

## 世界棲息地（2）

💡 閱讀原文：試用 3 分鐘的時間念完文章，記得先把中文遮上，並翻頁看題目問什麼。計時開始！

### World Habitats (2)

Neither as dry as deserts nor as **moist** as jungles, grasslands are most **abundant** in the temperate regions of the earth. Grasslands boast a wide **array** of wildlife, such as plants, insects, reptiles, birds, and a wide **assortment** of mammals. Savannas are tropical grasslands with trees, shrubs, and grasses that support exotic wildlife. The African savanna, for example, is home to herds of wildebeest, elephants, and gazelles, as well as black rhinoceros, giraffes, hippopotamuses, and lions.

Jungles support the greatest variety of plant and animal life on earth. Although they cover less than 6 percent of the world's land surface, these regions are the habitats for **innumerable** species of plants and animals. Their rainy, hot climate is ideal for supporting dense plant growth and large numbers of animals.

Because climate changes with **altitude**, a mountain can contain more than one ecological system. Mountains are the home of **predators**, such as snow leopards and golden eagles. These animals can coexist in a mountain setting with foragers, such as Himalayan ibexes and Alpine voles.

## 世界棲息地（2）

　　草原既不像沙漠那麼乾燥，也不像叢林那麼潮濕，在地球溫帶地區中面積十分遼闊。這裡野生動物種類繁多，像是植物、昆蟲、爬蟲、鳥、各式各樣的哺乳類。熱帶草原上面有樹、灌木、草，餵養著奇奇怪怪的野生動物。譬如説，非洲大草原棲息著一群群的牛羚、大象、蹬羚、黑犀牛、長頸鹿、河馬、獅子。

　　叢林裡物種之多居地球之冠。雖然僅覆蓋著世界 **6%**的表面，但是居住在這裡的物種數都數不清。炎熱多雨的氣候正適合大量動植物存活。

　　因為氣候會隨著高度而變化，因此一座山包含的生態系統可能不只一種。很多食肉動物都以高山為家，例如雪豹、金雕。這

些動物與巨角塔爾羊、高山野鼠這些覓食動物共存於高山環境裡。

## 考題演練及解析

**Which of the following best expresses the essential information in the underlined sentence? Incorrect answer choices change the meaning in important ways or leave out essential information.**

(A) Different from deserts or jungles, grasslands are mild in temperature.

(B) Unlike deserts or jungles, grasslands are rich in biodiversity.

(C) With the most abundant resources on earth, grasslands are not like deserts or jungles.

(D) Without such extremes of rainfall as deserts or jungles, grasslands are vast in area.

以下哪一句最能表達出劃底線句子的基本訊息？不正確的答案選項會以重要方式改變句義，或者遺漏基本訊息

(A) 跟沙漠、叢林不同，草原氣候上很溫和

(B) 不像沙漠、叢林，草原的生物多樣性很豐富

(C) 草原擁有地球上最豐盛的資源，跟沙漠、叢林不一樣

(D) 草原降雨量不像沙漠、叢林那麼極端，面積十分遼闊

👉 **解析**

答案｜**(D)**

❶ 這關鍵句前半段還不難理解，難懂的是後半段。abundant 意即「豐富的、充足的」，修飾的當然是前面的 grasslands，而不是下一句即將提到的 wildlife，更不是完全都沒出現的 resources ，因此 (B) (C) 選項都不對。

❷ (B) 選項的 biodiversity，字首 bio-「生物、生命」，後面 diversity 「多樣性」，合起來即草原「生物多樣性」非常 rich。很不幸，看看第二段第一句：
Jungles support the greatest variety of plant and animal life on earth.
這選項隨即慘遭打臉，因為就物種來說應該叫 jungle 第一名。

❸ abundant 修飾 grasslands 自然是指 grasslands 很多，所以要解讀成面積遼闊，答案非 (D) 莫屬。

從拆解自然、地理類題目，看連接詞的角色 1

## ⚙️ 深度應用分析：對付閱讀就是要化「繁」為「簡」。先刪去( )、[ ] 內的文字，找出主要的主詞和動詞！

**❶** [Neither (as dry as deserts) nor (as moist as jungles)], grasslands are most abundant (in the temperate regions of the earth).

### 👉 解析

**❶** 前半句是相關連接詞 neither A nor B 的對等結構，意即「既不 A 也不 B」、「A、B 都不……」。因為 neither A nor B = not + either A or B 所以不需要再加任何否定詞。分別置於句首連接兩個句子時，兩個句子都必須倒裝，例如：

Neither are students intelligent, nor are they diligent nowadays.

**❷** 後半句 grasslands are most abundant…的 most 因為前面沒有 the，所以並非最高級，而是應該做 very 解，亦即「非常廣大的」。例如：

It was most kind of you to come to the airport to see me off.

（你真好心到機場給我送行。）

I'll be most pleased to speak to them...

（能跟他們談談我會十分高興。）

❷ The African savanna, for example, is home to [herds of (wildebeest, elephants, and gazelles), as well as (black rhinoceros, giraffes, hippopotamuses, and lions)].

👉 **解析**

❶ 連接副詞 for example 只是語意上有承先啟後的作用，但是文法上並沒有連接的作用。**TOEFL 閱讀重視的是對整篇文章綱要的了解，而不是雞毛蒜皮。**一般 for instance、such、like 這些表示舉例的字眼，目的都是要讓讀者增進理解。因此除非考細節題，否則要是讀者都能抓住要點了，忽略這些末梢枝節也無傷大雅。就拿本文為例，最重要的內容幾乎都是每段第一、二句，提綱挈領點出大意後，其餘都是在介紹該生態區有哪些動物。即使不知道這些動物名稱，也不至於影響大局。

❷ 這句的 as well as 又是相關連接詞。和 neither A nor B 最大的差異是，A as well as B 的主詞是 A，動詞應該跟 A 一致；neither A nor B 的主詞是 B，動詞應該跟 B 一致。例如：Neither a leaf nor an insect stirred.（不單是樹葉，連隻蟲子都沒動）；My mother as well as I is satisfied with the result.（我媽跟我都滿意這樣的結果）。

從拆解自然、地理類題目，看連接詞的角色 1

# Gigantosaurus (1)

# 巨太龍（1）

 閱讀原文：試用 3 分鐘的時間念完文章，記得先把中文遮上，並翻頁看題目問什麼。計時開始！

### Gigantosaurus (1)

For many years, paleontologists thought that the Tyrannosaurus rex was the largest meat-eating dinosaur ever to **roam** the earth. In 1995, however, some bones were found in Argentina by an auto mechanic and **amateur** scientist named Ruben Carolini, whose discovery was to unseat Tyrannosaurus rex from its position as the largest meat-eating dinosaur. In honor of his discovery, scientists named the new dinosaur Gigantosaurus Carolini.

(A) After the initial find, scientists **exhumed** additional pieces of the Gigantosaurus skeleton, including parts of the skull, many of the vertebrae, both **thigh** bones, and some curved teeth, each of which was eight inches long and serrated like a saw. (B) From this incomplete skeleton, scientists were able to estimate the dinosaur's size and appearance. (C) According to researchers, the Gigantosaurus ran on its **hind** legs and had rather small arms. (D) The bones found so far indicate only part of one sample of Giganotosaurus, but are enough to classify it as a **distinct** species.

## 巨太龍（1）

許多年來，古生物學家都以為暴龍是橫行於地球上最大的肉食恐龍。然而在 1995 年，一位叫做 Ruben Carolini 的汽車師父兼業餘科學家發現了一堆骨頭，這發現使暴龍讓出了最大的肉食恐龍寶座。為紀念他的發現，科學家將這種新恐龍命名為 Gigantosaurus Carolini 巨太龍。

(A) 初步發現後，科學家挖出巨太龍另外骨架，包含部分頭蓋骨、許多椎骨、兩個大腿骨，一些彎曲牙齒，每顆牙齒都長達八英吋，有鋸子般的鋸齒。(B) 科學家可以從這不完整的骨架估計出這隻恐龍的大小樣子。(C) 根據研究人員所説，巨太龍用兩條後腿奔跑，手臂相當短。(D) 目前所發現的骨頭雖然顯示只是某個巨太龍的一部分，但是已經足以歸類為一種截然不同的物種。

ch 1
從拆解自然、地理類題目，看連接詞的角色 1

ch 2

ch 3

ch 4

ch 5

ch 6

Look at the four letters that indicate where the following sentence could be added to the passage.

**A bone-by-bone comparison with remains of the largest known specimen of Tyrannosaurus rex shows that the creature stood about 42 feet long, slightly taller than the Tyrannosaurus rex, and weighed six to eight tons, nearly three tons heavier than the largest Tyrannosaurus rex.**

Where could the sentence best fit?

看看文章裡四個字母，哪個地方可以把下面句子安插進去

「將骨頭拿來跟已知暴龍最大的標本逐一比對，可以發現這種生物高達 42 英呎，比暴龍略高，重達 6 到 8 公噸，幾乎比最大的暴龍還重 3 公噸。」

這句子放哪裡最合適？

### 解析

答案｜**(C)**

❶ 本文第一段介紹巨太龍的化石被發現的背景，第二段內容都是關於科學家對巨太龍化石的種種推測。

❷ 逐一瀏覽選項時，可以發現 (A) 不對，因為托福選文肯定是學術性論文，所以比起一般報刊雜誌文章而言，風格嚴謹講究邏輯，往往每段第一、二句就是主題句，而後再寫其他 supporting idea 來支持這個論點。本題這句話是比較巨太龍和暴龍的體型，內容上沒有主題句的氣勢，反而比較像是 supporting idea 之類的細節。

❸ 題目套進 (B) 時，跟前面第一句話的邏輯勉強還說得通，但是跟後面那句話顯然就搭不上了，因為不可能才剛講完巨太龍身高體重，下一句居然說科學家推測牠的大小與長相，顯然前後倒置。

❹ 把題目句接在 From this incomplete skeleton, scientists were able to estimate the dinosaur's size and appearance.後面不只邏輯順序很正確，而且隨後又緊接著介紹姿態長相，整個天衣無縫，因此答案就是 (C)。

❺ (D) 選項顯然遠不及 (C)，也沒必要再浪費時間比對。

## 深度應用分析：對付閱讀就是要化「繁」為「簡」。先刪去( )、[ ] 內的文字，找出主要的主詞和動詞！

❶ A bone-by-bone comparison (with remains of the largest known specimen of Tyrannosaurus rex) shows that [the creature stood about 42 feet long, (slightly taller than the Tyrannosaurus rex), and weighed six to eight tons, (nearly three tons heavier than the largest Tyrannosaurus rex)].

### 👉 解析

❶ 看到這麼長的句子，千萬不要慌了手腳，像本句長歸長，但是把一堆括號內的介系詞片語和補述用法全部去掉，可以發現只剩下赤裸裸關於巨太龍身高體重的描述。而那堆括號內的介系詞片語幾乎清一色關於暴龍的身高體重，顯然是拿暴龍來跟巨太龍做體型上的比較。

❷ 從屬連接詞 that 引領中括號裡的從屬子句作為 shows 的受詞，這種場合 that 可以省略。可是假如 that 帶領的從屬子句是當主詞時，就不能省略，例如：

That honesty is the best policy is beyond doubt.

（誠實為上策這個道理不容置疑。）

❷ In 1995, however, some bones were found in Argentina by an auto mechanic and amateur scientist [named Ruben Carolini, (whose discovery was to unseat Tyrannosaurus rex from its position as the largest meat-eating dinosaur).]

### 解析

❶ 這句子長度也不遑多讓。插入句題型作答時，最重要的是抓住題目句子的大意，而一個句子的大意幾乎都是其主要結構。只注意到細節，卻忽略掉大意，反而妨礙正確答案的判斷。

❷ named 前面原本有 who was，但是因為 who 跟 was 實際都沒有語意，因此省略，這是一種補述用法，例如：

Our school, located in the downtown area, offers some courses to the community.（我們學校坐落在市中心，也對社區開了一些課程）**提點**：這句話的 located 前面省略掉 which is。

❸ 後面關係子句雖然不屬於主要子句，但是所傳達的訊息卻十分重要，也就是先推翻學術界原先認為暴龍是塊頭最大的肉食恐龍這種論調。

從拆解自然、地理類題目，看連接詞的角色 1

CH 1

CH 2

CH 3

CH 4

CH 5

CH 6

# Gigantosaurus (2)

## 巨太龍（2）

 閱讀原文：試用 3 分鐘的時間念完文章，記得先把中文遮上，並翻頁看題目問什麼。計時開始！

### Gigantosaurus (2)

Scientists do not know exactly what the Gigantosaurus ate, but its teeth have all the **attributes** of meat-eating animals, so they have concluded that the great beast was a **carnivore**. Because skeletal remains of dinosaurs do not include skin, scientists must theorize about the dinosaurs' skin colors. A Gigantosaurus hunted smaller **prey**, so it is likely that the appearance of its skin allowed it to **blend** into its surroundings in order to surprise its **victims**. The Gigantosaurus lived in the grassy wetlands of what is now Argentina, an environment similar to the African savanna; therefore, this dinosaur probably had skin that closely matched the colors of the vegetation around it.

The Gigantosaurus Carolini lived about 100 million years ago, some 30 million years before the Tyrannosaurus rex that roamed North America. Despite many similarities between the two creatures, scientists have stated that the two are not closely related and that each species developed independently.

## 巨太龍（2）

科學家不知道巨太龍到底吃什麼，但是它的牙齒具備所有肉食動物的特徵，因此他們的結論是這頭巨獸是肉食動物。因為恐龍遺骸並沒有皮膚，所以科學家只能推測膚色。既然巨太龍捕捉小型獵物，為了給那些冤大頭殺了個冷不防，很可能它的外皮可以融入環境中。巨太龍生活在目前阿根廷的綠草濕地裡，環境跟非洲大草原很類似，因此這種恐龍的膚色很可能跟四周植被顏色極為匹配。

巨太龍生活在大約一億年前，比橫行北美洲的暴龍還要早三千萬年。雖然這兩種生物有許多相似點，但是科學家說兩者血緣關係並不親密，而且還各自獨立發展。

**Which of the following best expresses the essential information in the underlined sentence? Incorrect answer choices change the meaning in important ways or leave out essential information.**

(A) The grassy swamps of Argentina were home to the Giganotosaurus, which was likely to have skin the same colors as the vegetation it fed on.

(B) The Giganotosaurus might have a cunning camouflage lest they fall prey to their predators in the grassy wetlands.

(C) Since the Giganotosaurus lived in the grasslands of Argentina, its color must have looked like that of the plants found there.

(D) Found in South America, the Giganotosaurus could change its skin color to match the surroundings to prevent itself from being noticed by its games.

以下哪一句最能表達出劃底線句子的基本訊息？不正確的答案選項會以重要方式改變句義，或者遺漏基本訊息

(A) 綠草茂密的阿根廷沼澤是巨太龍的棲息地，這種恐龍的膚色很可能跟它所吃的植物一模一樣。

(B) 巨太龍可能有很巧妙的偽裝以免淪為濕地掠食動物的獵物。

(C) 因為巨太龍住在阿根廷的草原裡，所以膚色大概會跟那裡的植物看起來很像。

(D) 巨太龍是在南美洲發現的，其皮膚可以隨環境變色以免被其獵物察覺。

## 解析

答案 | (C)

❶ 英文分號有連接詞的作用，加上後面連接副詞 therefore 呈現出因果關係。也就是説，因為巨太龍生長在草原環境裡，所以科學家推測膚色可能和當地植物雷同。本文第一句話就説從牙齒可以推斷巨太龍是肉食動物，可是 (A) 選項最後卻説它以植物為主食，陳述錯誤。 (B) 選項的 fall/be prey to 意即「為……所苦、被……捕食」。巨太龍之所以可能跟環境顏色一樣是為了捕獵其他動物，但是 (B) 選項反而説是為了不要被其他動物捕獵，完全相反。

❷ (C) 選項以連接詞 since 表達出因果關係，後面還用 must have p.p.表示推測，符合題目的邏輯，是正確答案。 (D) 最後那個 game 是「獵物」，而非「遊戲」。這選項把巨太龍描述成變色龍，不過全文根本沒看到這種説法。面對文字艱澀的閱讀測驗時，最忌諱忽略主旨，被細節耍得團團轉，甚至是完全沒提過的臆測。

ch 1

ch 2

ch 3

ch 4

ch 5

ch 6

從拆解自然、地理類題目，看連接詞的角色 1

❶ The Gigantosaurus lived in the grassy wetlands [of what is now Argentina, (an environment similar to the African savanna)]; therefore, this dinosaur probably had skin (that closely matched the colors of the vegetation around it).

👉 解析

❶ 分號可連結兩個語意關係密切的句子，假如後面又出現 therefore、however、moreover、in other words、in addition、for example 之類的連接副詞時，會更凸顯兩句之間的邏輯關係。

❷ 但是要注意連接副詞不算連接詞，並不具備文法上連接的功能，因此若非以句號或分號結束前句，就需要再搭配另一個連接詞。此外，由於連接副詞不算句子結構的一部分，所以常常要用逗號跟原句隔開。

❸ Argentina 後面的 an environment similar to the African savanna 是它的同位語，補充說明 Argentina 濕地跟非洲草原差不多。然後下一句便根據巨太龍生長環境來推測其膚色應該會跟非洲草原上的獅、豹一樣，可以融入週遭的植物顏

色，這樣才有助於捕捉獵物。

❷ Despite many similarities between the two creatures, scientists have stated [(that the two are not closely related) and (that each species developed independently).]

👉 **解析**

❶ despite 和 though 同義，但是卻是介系詞，跟 in spite of 一樣，因此後面只能接名詞片語。例如：She still enjoyed the trip despite the traffic.（雖然交通不理想，但那趟旅行她還是玩得蠻愉快的。）

❷ 後面兩個從屬連接詞 that 各自引領一個從屬子句作為 stated 的受詞，這時第一個 that 因為沒有意思，所以可以省略，但是第二個 that 雖然也沒有意思，但是卻可以提醒讀者第二個子句還是做為 stated 的受詞，而非另一句，在文法上有一定的指示功用，因此不能省略。

❸ 本文主角是巨太龍，但是前後多次提到暴龍，在作答過程中要很清楚兩者的異同，因為不管哪一種題型，這樣的題材都很好命題。由於 TOEFL iBT 不像過去紙筆作答，無法在題本上直接劃線做記號，但是會發給三張紙（不夠還可以舉手要），所以作答過程中，碰到類似這樣的內容，要邊作答，邊寫下要點。

CH 1

從拆解自然、地理類題目，看連接詞的角色 1

CH 2

CH 3

CH 4

CH 5

CH 6

# Isaac Newton's Laws of Motion (1)

## 牛頓運動定律（1）

閱讀原文試用 3 分鐘的時間念完文章，記得先把中文遮上，並翻頁看題目問什麼。計時開始！

### Isaac Newton's Laws of Motion (1)

Sir Isaac Newton possessed one of the **keenest** scientific intellects of his time. In spite of his brilliance, he was a **humble** person who always tried to **depreciate** his contributions to science, preferring instead to honor the scientists who had **preceded** him. He once remarked, "If I have seen further [than others], it is by standing upon the shoulders of Giants."

Newton is famous primarily for his laws describing motion. When the plague forced Cambridge University to shut down temporarily, Newton left the university and stayed for a time at his mother's farm. It was during this period that Newton **formulated** the three laws of motion, which reduce nearly all the motion we observe to concepts that are relatively simple, considering the complexities of physics. While there is no evidence to support the popular, but no doubt apocryphal, story that Newton discovered **gravity** when an apple fell on his head as he sat under a tree, it seems certain that observing falling objects caused Newton to think about the forces at work in the universe.

## 牛頓運動定律（1）

　　牛頓擁有他那時代最犀利的科學天分。儘管成就斐然，他這人卻很謙虛，總是貶低自己在科學上的貢獻，反而喜歡彰顯比他出道更早的科學家。他曾經說過：「如果說我看得 [ 比別人 ] 更遠，那是因為我站在巨人的肩膀上」

　　牛頓主要以闡述運動的定律聞名於世。當劍橋大學因黑死病不得不暫時停課時，牛頓離開大學在媽媽農場裡待了一段時間。就是在這期間，牛頓構想出運動三大定律，將我們所觀察到的所有運動簡化為相當簡單的概念，沒有物理學慣有的繁複。有個虛構卻廣為人知的故事說，牛頓坐在樹下時，一顆蘋果砸到他的頭，因而發現地心引力。雖然沒有證據足以為證，但是似乎可以肯定的是觀察掉落的物體讓牛頓想到宇宙中運作的力量。

**According to this passage, which is NOT true of Sir Isaac Newton?**

(A) Doubt has been cast on the authenticity of the story that Newton's three laws of motion owed their inspiration to a falling apple.

(B) Newton came up with the laws of motion during a break in his studies at Cambridge University

(C) Though one of the best physicists of his generation, Newton was so modest as to credit his scientific achievements to the work of scientists senior to him.

(D) Keeping a careful watch on something dropping motivated Newton to develop his theory of gravity.

根據本文，以下關於牛頓的敘述哪一個是不對的？

(A) 牛頓運動三大定律的靈感源自一顆掉下來的蘋果，這個故事的真實性受到質疑。

(B) 在劍橋大學研究停課期間，牛頓提出了運動定律。

(C) 雖然是當代最傑出的物理學家，牛頓卻謙虛到把自己的科學成就歸功於前輩的努力。

(D) 仔細觀察掉下來的東西讓牛頓靈光一閃，開展出了地心引力學說。

## 解析

答案 | (A)

❶ 要是沒看清楚，會誤以為選項 (A) 是正確敘述，其實不是，因為那個蘋果砸到頭的傳說是說牛頓因此想到「地心引力」，而不是「運動三大定律」。雖然本文主題確實是運動三大定律，但是不代表牛頓其它成就都不會提到，何況地心引力跟運動三大定律也風馬牛不相及。

❷ (B) 選項是正確陳述，因為根據第二段前兩句陳述，由於瘟疫肆虐導致劍橋大學不得不停課，牛頓正是住在母親農場裡，那時構想的運動定律成為牛頓最重要的學說。

❸ 第一段整段都是在談牛頓多麼謙虛，就算不懂 humble 這個字，從牛頓說 If I have seen further, it is by standing upon the shoulders of Giants 這句話，也可以推測牛頓這個人有不居功的雅量，因此 (C) 所述完全正確。

❹ (D) 選項跟整篇文章最後那一行完全吻合。也就是說，蘋果掉在牛頓頭上這說法固然不可信，但是觀察掉落的物體給牛頓地心引力學說臨門一腳這種說法倒是比較可取。

*ch* 1 從拆解自然、地理類題目，看連接詞的角色 1

*ch* 2

*ch* 3

*ch* 4

*ch* 5

*ch* 6

❶ While {there is no evidence to support the popular(, but no doubt apocryphal,) story [that Newton discovered gravity(when an apple fell on his head as he sat under a tree)]}, {it seems certain that (observing falling objects caused Newton to think about the forces at work in the universe.)}

👈 解析

❶ 連接詞 while 連接一個廣為流傳的謠傳，和一個似乎比較可信的說法。該注意的是…when an apple fell on his head as he sat …這句話的 when 並不是連接詞「當」，更不是疑問詞「什麼時候」，而是關係副詞，意即「在…的時候」；同樣這子句後面那個的 as 意思才是「當」。

❷ when、while、as 字義都是「當」，部分場合用法又雷同，很容易造成混淆。假如主要子句表示一個短暫性動作，附屬子句表示一個持續性動作時，三者都可用，本句的 as 就是這種情況。不過因為前面已經出現過 while、when，為避免讀者混淆，所以用 as。只有 while 可以表示對比並列，本句開頭第一個字 while 就是這種情況。假如主要子句和附屬子

句所表示的動作並非同時發生，而是有先後順序，一般都用 when，例如：When the clock strikes twelve, the girl must go home.（鐘敲 12 下時，這女孩就必須回家。）

❷ It was during this period that Newton formulated the three laws of motion, [which reduce nearly all the motion (we observe) to concepts (that are relatively simple, considering the complexities of physics.)]

👉 **解析**

❶ 這是 it is …that…強調句型，把 during this period 套進 it is 和 that 當中意味這是很重要的訊息，提醒讀者這段期間就是牛頓的運動三大定律誕生的搖籃。關係代名詞 which 引導的子句裡還有兩個關係子句：一句是 we observe，前面有 which，但是因為在附屬子句是受詞，所以省略掉了；另一句 concepts 後面的 that 子句，因為關係代名詞 that 在附屬子句是主詞，所以不能省略，但是可以改成 which。

❷ 本文 motion 出現很多次，其實英文很多 mo 開頭的字，都跟 move 有關，光大家最熟悉的就有 movie「電影」、motor「馬達」、mobile「行動的」，其它親戚像 **motive**「動機」、motif「動機」、**momentum**「動力」，還有遠親 **migrate**「遷移」，結構複雜一點的是 **commotion** = com(together、thoroughly) + mot + ion(名詞字尾) =「騷動」。

# Isaac Newton's Laws of Motion (2)

## 牛頓運動定律（2）

 閱讀原文：試用 **3** 分鐘的時間念完文章，記得先把中文遮上，並翻頁看題目問什麼。計時開始！

### Isaac Newton's Laws of Motion (2)

(A) Contrary to the popular belief that it was natural for moving objects to slow down and eventually stop moving, Newton stated that any change in the motion of an object was the result of a force.(B) A ball set in motion slows down and stops because of the force of **friction**. (C) Newton's First Law is **reinforced** whenever objects are sent into the almost frictionless environment of space. (D)

Newton's Second Law describes changes in speed: Acceleration is directly proportional to the amount of force applied and **inversely proportional** to mass. This law is important to engineers today as they work to increase the efficiency of automobiles. Perhaps because of its **brevity**,

Newton's Third Law is one of the most quoted: For every action there is an equal and opposite reaction. If you step off a boat that is not securely **moored**, the boat may move backward as much as you try to move forward. If your goal was to step on the dock, Newton's Third Law could leave you very wet.

## 牛頓運動定律（2）

（A）當時廣為接受的信念是，移動的物體速度會遞減，最後停止不動，這是天經地義的。牛頓的說法卻背道而馳，他說一個物體移動之所以產生變化都是外力使然。（B）處於運動中的球之所以減速停下來都是因為摩擦力的關係。（C）不管哪時候把東西投送到幾乎沒有摩擦力的太空環境中，牛頓第一定律都能得到證實。（D）

　　牛頓第二定律描述的是速度的變化：加速度和施力成正比，和質量成反比。這條定律對今天的工程師尤為重要，因為他們都想盡辦法要提升汽車的效率。或許因為簡潔的緣故，牛頓第三定律是最經常被引用的一個：每個相互作用都會有一股反作用力，大小相等、方向相反。要從沒栓好的船下來時，愈想往前動，船可能愈往後跑。假如以登上碼頭為目標的話，牛頓第三定律可能會讓你跌成落湯雞。

Look at the four letters that indicate where the following sentence could be added to the passage.

**If a frictionless environment were available, a moving object could theoretically stay in motion forever.**

Where could the sentence best fit?

看看文章裡四個字母，哪個地方可以把下面句子安插進去

假如在沒有摩擦力的環境下，一個移動的物體就理論來說會永遠一直處於運動狀態。

這句子放哪裡最合適？

 解析

答案｜(C)

❶ 英文凡是闡述真理、定律，一律用現在式來表示其永恆不變的狀態；凡是提到歷史事件，一律用過去式來表示其已成既定事實。前一篇文章談牛頓的生平，由於都是陳年往事，因此幾乎一路過去式到底。本文開始介紹到牛頓三大運動定律，因此從第二句話開始，時式從過去式轉變成現在式。

❷ 條件子句主詞 a frictionless environment 明明是單數，但是動詞卻是 were，證明這是與現在事實相反假設，這是一

條極為重要的線索。

❸ TOEFL 的文章結構都很嚴謹，每段第一、二句往往是主題句，顧名思義一定會簡明扼要說明整個段落的精華。這個特點在插入句題型蠻管用的，因為只要題目欠缺主題句的大家風範，絕對不可能放在每段開頭第一句，選項 (A) 正是如此。假設法主要用來陳述某種條件下的可能性，先天上就欠缺切中要害的功能。

❹ 以關鍵字 friction 來搜尋，題目套進 (C) 上下文邏輯正好吻合。

❶ If (a frictionless environment were available), (a moving object could theoretically stay in motion forever.)

👉 解析

❶ 這句話是連接詞 if 所構成的與現在事實相反假設語氣。既然是與現在事實相反假設，就意味這句話的陳述就目前來看不是真的。也就是說，在目前環境下根本不可能沒有磨擦力，所以移動中的物體也不可能永遠處於運動狀態。

❷ 凡是與現在事實相反的假設，be 動詞一律用 were。該注意的是，假設語氣可以省略 if，但是省略掉以後，條件子句的助動詞或 be 動詞就要搬到句首形成倒裝。因此這一句話也可以寫成：Were a frictionless environment available, a moving object could theoretically stay in motion forever.

❸ 提到未來，有三種情況，茲舉三例說明，每句意思都是「假如他有一百萬，她就嫁給他」
   ◆ If he has one million dollars, she will marry him. 這種說法是蠻有可能的

◆ If he should have one million dollars, she would marry him. 這種說法雖然也有可能，但是機率不高

◆ If he were to have one million dollars, she would marry him. 這種說法是完全不可能，機率是零

❷ [Contrary to the popular belief (that it was natural for moving objects to slow down and eventually stop moving)], Newton stated (that any change in the motion of an object was the result of a force.)

### 👉 解析

❶ contrary 意即「相反的」，這句話透過 Contrary to the popular belief 這個片語作為主要子句主詞 Newton 的補述用法，強調牛頓的信念與大家南轅北轍，在當時算是異類。

❷ Contrary to the popular belief that…的 that 從屬連接詞所帶領的名詞子句是 the popular belief 的同位語，亦即告訴讀者所謂 the popular belief 就是指 it was natural for moving objects to slow down and eventually stop moving 這種想法。

❸ contrary 和 **contrast**「對比、對照」的字首都是 contra-，更常見是拼成 counter-，意即 against，例如 **counterattack**「反攻」、**counterclockwise**「逆時鐘方向」。

# Charting the Elements (1)

## 元素週期表（1）

閱讀原文：試用 **3** 分鐘的時間念完文章，記得先把中文遮上，並翻頁看題目問什麼。計時開始！

### Charting the Elements (1)

Throughout history, people have wondered about the **composition** of the earth and of the air around them. Aristotle held that everything was made of four **substances** - earth, air, fire, and water. This belief persisted for more than two thousand years; however, when this theory was examined scientifically, it was shown to be unfounded.

In the fourth and fifth centuries, alchemy, a **peculiar** combination of myth, magic, and science, began to gain **prominence**. Many of the alchemists' efforts were devoted to a **futile** search for a method of turning common metals into gold. Although such efforts seem rather far removed from science as we know it today, some scientific knowledge was eventually **extrapolated** from alchemy.

The ascendancy of modern chemistry didn't begin until the French chemist Antoine Lavoisier established the law of conservation of mass. One of the first to see patterns in the reactions of elements was a German chemist named Dobereiner, who noted that certain elements with similar properties occurred in groups of threes, which he called triads. Dobereiner's rudimentary observations set off a search for more relationships.

## 元素週期表（1）

有史以來，人類就一直想知道地球與自己週遭空氣的成分。亞里斯多德認為所有一切都是由四種物質構成——地、風、火、水。這種信念延續了兩千年，然而用科學來檢驗這理論時，便顯得毫無事實根據。

煉金術是揉合神話、魔法、科學的一種怪異組合，在第四、第五世紀時開始嶄露頭角。這些煉金術士諸多心血都投入於對煉金術夸父逐日般的追求。雖然這些努力似乎跟我們今天所知道的科學相去甚遠，但是最後某些科學知識卻是從煉金術中淬煉出來。

一直到法國化學家拉瓦節確立質量守恆定律以後，現代化學

從拆解自然、地理類題目，看連接詞的角色 1

才開始風行起來。第一位從元素反應中看出規則的是一位叫做貝萊納的德國化學家，他注意到具備類似屬性的某些元素正好三個三個一組，他將之命名為「三元素組」。 貝萊納初步的觀察開啟了更多元素之間關係的探索。

## 📝 考題演練及解析

**Which of the following best expresses the essential information in the underlined sentence? Incorrect answer choices change the meaning in important ways or leave out essential information.**

(A) The study of the structure of matter took a turn from philosophy to science after Antoine Lavoisier developed the law of conservation of mass.

(B) Chemistry has been part of everything in daily life since the law of conservation of mass was proposed.

(C) By the time Antoine Lavoisier discovered the law of conservation of mass, chemistry had risen to popularity among scientists.

(D) The study of substances did not come into being until the establishment of the law of conservation of mass.

以下哪一句最能表達出劃底線句子的基本訊息？不正確的答案選項會以重要方式改變句義，或者遺漏基本訊息。

(A) 物質結構的研究在拉瓦節提出能量守恆定律後，才從哲學轉向科學。

(B) 自從能量守恆定律提出以後，化學就成為日常生活的一部分。

(C) 到了拉瓦節發現能量守恆定律時，化學已很受科學家歡迎了。

(D) 直到能量守恆定律確立以後，物質的研究才開始出現。

### 解析

答案 | (A)

❶ ascendancy 是 ascend 的名詞。ascend 是「上升、爬坡」，爬上去以後，便佔有制高點，因此名詞 ascendancy 引申為「優勢」。

❷ 這句話意思是「直到法國化學家拉瓦節確立質量守恆定律後，現代化學才開始佔上風」。因為化學源自古代煉金術，因此一直跟哲學密不可分，這從第一、二段內容就看得出來。要到拉瓦節提出質量守恆定律後，化學裡科學、哲學的比重開始先翻轉，科學逐漸取代哲學，化學完成華麗轉身。因此答案是 (A)。

❶ (The ascendancy of modern chemistry didn't begin) until (the French chemist Antoine Lavoisier established the law of conservation of mass).

## 解析

❶ 從屬連接詞 until 沒有和 not 連用的例句有

——I looked at her until the teacher came in.（我一直注視著她，直到老師進來。）

❷ not 連用的例句有

——I did not see her until the teacher came in.（我一直到老師進來，才看到老師。）

❸ 本句動詞 begin 是説一件事 begin 以後，和 not 連用後，就是指這個動作就無法繼續下去。

❷ One of the first to see patterns in the reactions of elements was a German chemist {named Dobereiner, [who noted that certain elements with similar properties occurred in groups of threes, (which he called triads)]}.

### 👉 解析

❶ 這句話主要子句就從開頭到 a German chemist 為止，後面則一段一段每段都用關係子句修飾下去，愈拉愈長，主要是在講 貝萊納這位德國化學家是化學史上第一位看出不同元素之間具備類似屬性這套規律的第一人。

❷ 這句話的 pattern 應該解讀成 way in which something happens「模式」，也就是化學元素反應的一套模式、一種規律

❸ proper 有兩個常見的意思，一個是「專屬的」，例如 proper noun「專有名詞」，名詞 property 是指專屬某個人的「財產」或專屬某個東西的「屬性」；專為某個人打造專屬的東西，肯定會非常適合這人的條件、期待……，因此 proper 另一個意思就是「適合的、適當的」。

# Charting the Elements (2)

# 元素週期表（2）

閱讀原文：試用 **3** 分鐘的時間念完文章，記得先把中文遮上，並翻頁看題目問什麼。計時開始！

### Charting the Elements (2)

In 1866 an English chemist named Newlands proposed his law of octaves, which **superseded** Dobereiner's triads. With the discovery that certain characteristics reappeared with every eighth element provided that elements were arranged in order of weight, Newlands could now predict the properties of a **hypothetical** element even before it was discovered.

Three years later a Russian scientist, Dmitri Mendeleev, **refined** Newland's observations. Mendeleev also had observed that certain properties seemed to recur on a regular basis. His special contribution, however, was his unique way of demonstrating this cycle. Without resorting to scientific lingo or confusing mathematics, he devised a chart of the elements, arranged in order of weight, that could be understood by almost anyone. Moreover, he took the unusual step of leaving certain parts of the chart blank. An empty place indicated that an element of a certain weight and property existed theoretically, but to date such an element had not been found. Mendeleev was honored as the father of the periodic table. A **crater** on the moon is named after him, as is element number 101, **radioactive** Mendelevium.

## 元素週期表（2）

1866 年一位叫做紐蘭茲的英國化學家提出了「元素八音律」，取代了 貝萊納的「三元素組」，也就是只要元素按照原子量來排列，每逢第八個元素都會出現某些特性。根據這發現，即使在還沒找到某個假設的元素以前，紐蘭茲就能預測其屬性。

三年後，一位俄羅斯科學家門得列夫改進了紐蘭茲的看法。門得列夫也觀察到某些特性似乎會很有規律地重複出現，而他最特殊的貢獻就是展現這種週期的獨門方式。完全沒靠科學術語或令人費解的數學，他按照原子量來排列，設計出一套大家都看得懂的元素週期表。此外，他還採用了一種非比尋常的作法，那就是將圖表中某些部分留白。留白的地方表示具備某一種原子量與特性的元素就理論上來說應該存在，但是當時卻還沒發現。門得

列夫被尊為週期表之父。月球上有個隕石坑就是以他的名字來命名，還有第 101 號放射性元素「鍆」也是。

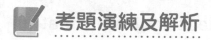 **考題演練及解析**

**According to this passage, which is NOT true of Dmitri Mendeleev?**

(A) The scientist created a periodic table that could accurately predict the properties of elements that had yet to be discovered.

(B) As Charles Darwin is to the theory of evolution, so is Dmitri Mendeleev to the periodic table.

(C) We named a kind of element in honor of the scientist.

(D) He was the first person to propose the existence of periodicity as a chemical property of the different elements.

根據這篇文章，關於門得列夫，哪一個說法是不對的？

(A) 這科學家設計出一份週期表，可以精確預測尚未發現元素的特性。

(B) 達爾文之於進化論，就好比門得列夫之於週期表。

(C) 我們以這科學家名字來為一種元素命名以彰紀念。

(D) 他是提出不同元素的化學屬性存在著規律的第一人。

# 解析

答案 | (D)

❶ 這一題的關鍵句是第一段的最後一句話 With the discovery…before it was discovered。從這句話可以得知紐蘭茲提出元素八音律時，甚至前文提到的 貝萊納的三元素組時，就已經推測出不同元素的化學屬性存在著一種規律，因此這一題答案是 (D)。

❷ (B) 選項的句型 As…so…「正如……一樣；……也是如此」，這是一種表示「類比」的句型，其中 as 是連接詞，意思是「像……一樣」，so 意思是「如此」，例如：Water is to fish as sunshine is to flowers.（正如水之於魚一樣，陽光之於花朵也是如此。）

❸ 從第二段倒數第二、第三句可以得知 (A) 選項敘述正確無誤。雖然紐蘭茲早一步宣稱可以預測尚未發現元素的特性，但是門得列夫的週期表也可以，邏輯上並沒有衝突。

❹ 最後一句話可以佐證 (C) 選項正確。其中…as is element number 101, radioactive Mendelevium 的 as 也可以改成 so，注意這種場合一定要倒裝。

❶ With the discovery [that (certain characteristics reappeared with every eighth element) provided (that elements were arranged in order of weight)], Newlands could now predict the properties of a hypothetical element (even before it was discovered).

👉 解析

❶ 這句話的 provided 是連接詞，後面的 that 可以省略不寫，功用是連接 certain characteristics reappeared with every eighth element 和 elements were arranged in order of weight 這兩句，意思是「假如、在…情況下」，常常用在正式文件之中。此外，provided (that)也可以寫成 providing(that)，類似的字眼還有 suppose (that)、supposing (that)、on condition (that)，意思都和 if 差不多。例如：

• Suppose you have one million dollars, what would you do?（如果你有一百萬元，會怎麼辦？）
• Provided (that) it is fine tomorrow, I'll go camping.（如果明天天氣好，我就去露營。）

❷ provided 連接的這兩句用中括號圈起來，這部分就是前面 discovery 的同位語，用來說明紐蘭茲的發現就是中括號裡面的內容，亦即紐蘭茲發現，假如按照原子量來排列，每逢第八個元素就會出現某種特性。憑藉著這個發現，他就能預測某個元素的屬性，哪怕這元素還沒被發現都能。

❷ An empty place indicated [(that an element of a certain weight and property existed theoretically), but (to date such an element had not been found)].

## 👉 解析

❶ 用中括號圈起來的部分就是指門得列夫週期表某些欄位故意留白，乃是意有所指。

❷ to date 的 to 並非不定詞，這片語意思是「迄今」，等於 so far、up to now/then，因此動詞時式常常要用完成式，例如：This is the biggest donation they've had to date.（這是到目前為止他們所收到的最大一筆捐贈。）

❸ indicate 源自 dic(t)字根，意思是 say，可是有話要說不一定會開口，也可以靠肢體語言比手劃腳，其中又以 index finger「食指」最重要，因為指東西時最常常用到這根指頭，甚至連指示符號也以「☞」伸出食指最常見。同理，indicate 字義是「指示」。

# Roses from Far Away (1)

## 來自遠方的玫瑰（1）

 閱讀原文：試用 3 分鐘的時間念完文章，記得先把中文遮上，並翻頁看題目問什麼。計時開始！

**Roses from Far Away (1)**

Have you ever considered how a **bunch** of red roses got to you? It is a **remarkable** process because most of the roses in florists or supermarkets in England have travelled hundreds, if not thousands, of miles. The world's number one producer of roses for Britain is currently Kenya.

In Kenya, most of the flower farms are in the **Rift** Valley that supplies the water. It has an ideal climate and lots of cheap labor. Favorable as the climate is, most flowers are produced in greenhouses to protect them from the occasional hailstorm or from becoming wet before they are harvested. Wet flowers rot quickly, so they need to be picked while the blooms are dry. Having them indoors also facilitates spraying and **pest** control. Picking them at the right time is **crucial**.

Once the flowers are picked it is a race against time. They are boxed without water, cooled to keep them as fresh as possible, and taken from the farms to the **hub** at Nairobi and then almost anywhere in the Britain within 48 hours of being cut.

### 來自遠方的玫瑰（1）

你曾經想過一束紅玫瑰是怎麼到達你手上的嗎？這過程頗值得關注，因為英格蘭花店或超市裡大部分玫瑰，要不是來自幾千，不然就是幾百英哩以外。目前英國玫瑰第一大生產國是肯亞。

肯亞大部分花田都位在有水源供應的東非大裂谷。那裡氣候很合適，勞動力也很低廉。儘管氣候宜人，大部分花朵還是種在溫室裡好好保護，以免慘遭雹災或者在採收前不幸淋濕。淋濕的花朵爛得很快，所以必須趁花朵還很乾時，趕緊採收。把它們養在室內也有助於農藥噴灑與害蟲控制。算準花朵採收時間事關重大。

花朵一摘下來，就開始和時間展開競賽。它們在無水情況下裝箱、冷藏，儘可能保持新鮮，從農場送到奈洛比的集散中心，然後在採收後 48 小時內送到全英各地。

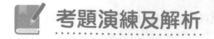

The author states that most of Kenya's exported flowers are grown in greenhouses for all of the following reasons EXCEPT

(A) it keeps the flowers dry before they are cut.

(B) it protects the plants from heat so that they won't wither easily.

(C) it provides the plants with shelters in case of violent weather.

(D) it makes it easier to sprinkle the flowers with a chemical to kill harmful insects.

作者說肯亞大部分要出口的花都種在溫室裡，以下何者並非其因素？

(A) 這樣可以讓花朵在收成以前保持乾燥。

(B) 這樣可以讓植物隔熱，以免枯萎掉。

(C) 這樣可以遮蔽植物，以防天氣惡劣。

(D) 這樣給花朵噴灑農藥殺死害蟲會容易一些

**解析**

答案｜(B)

❶ 解題的關鍵就在第二段的中後段，亦即

…most flowers are produced in greenhouses to protect them from the occasional hailstorm or from becoming wet…

這一句的不定詞 to 是表目的的 in order to，答案很明顯就在這裡，由此可知因素涵蓋 (A) (C) 選項。

可是再跳過一句 Having them indoors also facilitates spraying and pest control. 之後，這裡又說明另一個原因，由此可知 (D) 選項也是其中一個因素。既然是選出唯一例外的答案，因此答案是 (B)。

❷ 第二段前前後後出現 hailstorm、wet、dry、spray、pest 這些字眼，應該可以大膽做出預測：

hailstorm 跟 (C) 選項有關；wet、dry 跟 (A) 選項有關；spray、pest 跟 (D) 選項有關；只有 (B) 選項是孤兒，因為全文都沒提到跟其內容沾上邊的 hot、cold、wither、die…。

❸ (C) 選項的 in case of 意即「假如、萬一」，經常是用在事情還沒發生，先防範於未然。例如：

Ring the bell in case of emergency.

（萬一有急事就按鈴。）

Have everything ready just in case.

（把一切準備好以防萬一。）

## ⚙️ 深度應用分析：對付閱讀就是要化「繁」為「簡」。先刪去( )、[ ] 內的文字，找出主要的主詞和動詞！

**❶** Favorable as the climate is, most flowers are produced in greenhouses [to protect them (from the occasional hailstorm) or (from becoming wet before they are harvested)].

### 👉 解析

**❶** 連接詞 as 在這種倒裝句型應該做「雖然」解。可以放在句首的不是只有形容詞而已，舉凡副詞、名詞、動詞都能。例如：

- Hard as he tried, he failed.（雖然很認真嘗試，他還是失敗了。）

- Much as I wanted to talk, I kept silent.（雖然我很想講點話，但還是保持沉默。）

- Try as I would, I couldn't open the box.（不管我怎麼試，都打不開這盒子。）

- Man as he was, he is more beautiful than any women.（雖然他是男人，卻比任何女人還要貌美。）**提點**：名詞在句首時，不用加冠詞 a(n)。

❷ 中括號框起來的 to 不定詞片語表目的，裡面的 or 連接兩個 from 介系詞片語，說明把花種在溫室裡目的就是要避免 the occasional hailstorm 冰雹與 becoming wet before they are harvested 弄濕兩大危害。

❷ (Having them indoors) also facilitates spraying and pest control.

### 📖 解析

❶ once 是連接詞，連接括弧框起來的兩個句子，意思是「一旦」，等於 as soon as、the moment。例如：Once the flowers are picked, it is a race against time.
= As soon as the flowers are picked, it is a race against time.
= The moment the flowers are picked, it is a race against time.

❷ 「一……就……」還可以用 no sooner…than… 或 scarcely…when…表達，但是時式上沒有 as soon as、the mement 那麼隨和，常常要用過去式和過去完成式，所以要特別注意兩句的時間先後順序。因為 no sooner…than… 和 scarcely…when… 對時式比較講究，所以本句 Once the flowers are picked, it is a race against time 無法用這兩種句型改寫。

# Roses from Far Away (2)

## 來自遠方的玫瑰（2）

💡 閱讀原文：試用 3 分鐘的時間念完文章，記得先把中文遮上，並翻頁看題目問什麼。計時開始！

### Roses from Far Away (2)

(A) However, the majority of flowers go to Aalsmeer market, the biggest flower market in the world, just outside Amsterdam. It has one million square meters of warehouse space and up to twenty million flowers a day are sold there. (B) Wholesalers **bid** for them: prices start high and then are lowered - the classic Dutch **auction**. (C) They are rushed to the UK by plane or in **refrigerated** trucks and are delivered to florists. (D)

But what does this mean for the environment and the carbon footprint involved in transporting flowers for such large distances? Surprisingly, research carried out by Cranfield University discovered that roses grown by the

Dutch had a carbon footprint six times higher than those produced in Kenya. But what does this mean for the environment and the carbon footprint involved in transporting flowers for such large distances? Surprisingly, research carried out by Cranfield University discovered that roses grown by the Dutch had a carbon footprint six times higher than those produced in Kenya. This is because growing roses need **vast** amounts of energy, mainly sun and heat, which is free and **plentiful** in Kenya, while in Holland, it has to be provided by other means.

### 來自遠方的玫瑰（2）

(A) 然而大部分花朵都是送到阿爾斯梅爾市場上，這市場在阿姆斯特丹的外圍，是世界上最大的花市，擁有一百萬平方公尺的倉庫空間，每天在那裏賣掉的花高達兩千萬朵。(B) 批發商競標時，價碼從高喊到低，這就是典型的荷蘭式拍賣。(C) 這些花用飛機或冷凍貨車火速送到英國去，再轉送到各花店。(D)

可是將這些花轉送到千里之外，對環境與碳足跡是代表什麼意義呢？令人訝異的是，克蘭菲大學所做的研究卻顯示荷蘭種植的玫瑰產生的碳足跡是肯亞的六倍。這是因為玫瑰所需要的熱與光需要大量的能源，這些能源在肯亞既免費又取之不竭，可是在荷蘭卻必須以其他方式來提供。

Look at the four letters that indicate where the following sentence could be added to the passage.

**It will not be long before wholesalers buy these flowers and then re-export them to other markets across the globe.**

Where could the sentence best fit?

看看文章裡四個字母，哪個地方可以把下面句子安插進去

不久批發商會買下這些花，然後再將它們出口到世界其他市場。

這句子放哪裡最合適？

### 解析

答案 | (C)

❶ 一般來説，假如插入題型的題目出現 it、he、them 之類的代名詞或 this、those、here 之類的指示詞，恭喜你，這是天上掉下來的禮物！因為只要透過上下文，把代名詞或指示詞的本尊揪出來，拼湊出邏輯順序，答案很快會呼之欲出。

❷ 不過看到這一題一開頭就是 It，可不要高興得太早，因為這個 It 是代表時間，就好比 What time is it 的 it 並不是取代前後文之中哪一個名詞。

❸ 儘管如此，也用不著垂頭喪氣，因為根據常識就知道花果蔬菜一摘下來，保鮮期限就開始倒數，不得不與時間展開競賽，遠從肯亞千里而來，當然是要賣錢的。何況連題目都出現 wholesaler 這字眼，就知道批發商進場了。

❹ 即使不認識 wholesaler，但是從題目 buy、re-export 這些字眼，也能判斷這些花開始進入市場了，而且即將轉運到其他地方，把答案塞進 (C) 這位置正好跟前後文天衣無縫。

## ⚙ 深度應用分析：對付閱讀就是要化「繁」為「簡」。先刪去( )、[] 內的文字，找出主要的主詞和動詞！

❶ (It will not be long) before (wholesalers buy these flowers and then re-export them to other markets across the globe).

### 解析

❶ 表時間先後的連接詞 before 連接兩句，注意
it will not be long before… = before long = soon。例如：
It was not long before they were deep in conversation
= Before long, they were deep in conversation.
（不久他們就聊得很起勁了。）

❷ 這句話意思是說在荷蘭大批發市場裡批發商火速標下這些花轉運到其他各地方，可是拍賣方式卻很有意思。一般 auction「拍賣」，大家競標時數字都是愈開愈「大」，但是 Dutch auction 卻是愈喊愈低，其實台灣果菜批發市場也是這

❸ auction 這字「大」有來歷，它的家世背景會令你肅立起敬：augment「增強、擴大」、august「威嚴的」、authority「權威」。還有 author「作家」！

❷ Surprisingly, research (carried out by Cranfield University) discovered [that roses (grown by the Dutch) had a carbon footprint six times higher than those (produced in Kenya)].

👉 解析

❶ 副詞 surprisingly 放句首修飾逗點後面整句，也就是這所大學的研究結果讓大家跌破眼鏡。凡是修飾整句的副詞一定要放句首，也要用逗點和句子隔開。例如：Frankly, I lose confidence in her.（老實說，我對她失去信心了。）

❷ 後面的 those 是 roses 的代名詞，也就是拿荷蘭所種的玫瑰跟肯亞所種的玫瑰來做比較。要注意同類的東西才能比較，即「人對人」或「物對物」，例如：The climate of Kaohsiung is much hotter than that of Taipei.（高雄氣候比台北熱很多。）

❸ 你可能對 carbon footprint 的認識是零，但是從 carbon「碳」和前一句的 environment、後一句的 energy、heat，應該可以猜得出來跟環保有關。所謂 carbon footprint 就是一個活動或產品的整個生命週期過程所直接與間接產生的溫室效應氣體排放量。就距離來看，肯亞玫瑰遠從千里而來，於理來說排放的二氧化碳應該遠高於荷蘭玫瑰，但事實卻非如此。

# The Innovators (1)

## 創新者（1）

 閱讀原文：試用 3 分鐘的時間念完文章，記得先把中文遮上，並翻頁看題目問什麼。計時開始！

### The Innovators (1)

Invention is one thing, but innovation, the ability of transforming an invention into a commercially **viable** product, is another. Many businesses have played their part in the development of the motor car. However, two great innovating companies stand out from the rest. The first is Ford which brought it to a mass market, and the second Toyota that has become a **benchmark** of quality and reliability that all car manufacturers try to **emulate**.

While Karl Benz invented the first petrol driven vehicle in 1885, it needed the organizational and production innovations of the great car maker Henry Ford to turn it into a mode of transport and an object of consumer **aspiration** for ordinary people. Ford's use of a moving **assembly** line, where one worker concentrated on a particular task, allowed his company to achieve efficiencies and economies of scale that meant a car came off the production line every fifteen minutes. Such was Ford's success that by 1918 half the cars on the road were Model T Fords, which even an ordinary worker could afford.

### 創新者（1）

發明是一回事，但是創新又是另一回事，而創新就是將發明轉換成商業上確實可行商品的能力。在汽車研發過程中，許多企業都扮演著自己的角色，然而這當中有兩家偉大的創新公司脫穎而出，第一個就福特，它引領汽車走向大眾市場；第二個是豐田，它在品質與可靠度上已經成為所有汽車製造商爭相仿傚的基準。

1885 年卡爾賓士發明第一部汽油驅動的車輛時，所需要的就是亨利福特這種偉大汽車製造商的組織、生產創新力，將車輛轉變成一種運輸模式以及普羅大眾渴望購買的一種東西。福特使用移動式裝配線，在這種方式下，一位工人只專注於一項工作，讓他的公司發揮出驚人的效能與規模經濟，這意味每隔 15 分鐘生產線就組裝出一部汽車。福特是這麼成功，以至於到了 1918 年，街上一半汽車都是福特 T 型車，這種車甚至連一個普通工人都買得起。

**Which of the following best expresses the essential information in the underlined sentence? Incorrect answer choices change the meaning in important ways or leave out essential information.**

(A) Ford was considerably successful so that the Model T sold like hot cakes.

(B) The Ford factory successfully installed an assembly line to make it easy for the workers to mass-produce its best-selling product, the Model T.

(C) Because the Model T was financially available to a majority of Americans, Ford enjoyed enormous success.

(D) Ford's mass production system functioned so successfully that the Model T could be sold at a price acceptable to most Americans.

以下哪一句最能表達出劃底線句子的基本訊息？不正確的答案選項會以重要方式改變句義，或者遺漏基本訊息

(A) 福特極為成功，目的就是要讓 T 型車熱賣

(B) 福特工廠成功安裝了裝配線，目的就是要讓工人輕鬆地大量生產它最暢銷的 T 型車

(C) 因為大部分美國人都買得起 T 型車，福特大大成功了

(D) 福特大量生產系統運作得如此成功，以至於 T 型車能夠以大多數美國人可接受的價格傾銷

### 解析

答案｜(D)

❶ 這是 such/so…that 表結果的倒裝句型，注意這是有因果關係的，也就是 that 之前表「因」，that 之後表「果」。例如：So great was the suggestion that he was rewarded. （這建議這麼好，他因而得到獎勵。）言下之意就是——因為他提出的建議很棒，所以才得到獎勵此外還要注意 such 是限定詞，亦即它會跟前面提過的名詞有關。根據本文，such 是指 assembly line 這件事。因此題目這句話是指，因為福特引入裝配線得以大量生產成功，所以街上跑的汽車一半是 T 型車，幾乎大家都買得起。

❷ (A) 選項的…so that…句型是表「目的」，跟題目表因果的 so…that…截然不同；(B) 選項後面…line to make it easy…的第一個 to 是表目的的 in order to，…for the worker to mass-produce…的第二個 to 是 make 真正的受詞，前面的 it 就是它的虛受詞。這句話沒有抓住原句精髓。

❸ 附屬子句為人人都買得起的原因 (Because)，主要子句則寫福特成功的結果，但事實上並非如此，人人買得起的車是結果，因此 (C) 選項倒果為因。

❹ (D) 選項只是把原來 such 改寫成 so，原句型幾乎沒變，所以這就是標準答案。

## ⚙️ 深度應用分析：對付閱讀就是要化「繁」為「簡」。先刪去( )、[ ] 內的文字，找出主要的主詞和動詞！

❶ Such was Ford's success that [by 1918 half the cars on the road were Model T Fords, (which even an ordinary worker could afford)].

👉 解析

❶ such 和 so 最大的差異是──such 是形容詞，修飾名詞；so 是副詞，修飾形容詞或其他副詞。注意凡是複數名詞或不可數名詞一定是用 such，除非後面接 many 或 much，這時就只能用 so。例如：

- These children's books are a real bargain at such low prices.（這些童書價格這麼便宜，真划得來。）
- Such hot weather in August is beyond example in this area.（八月份這麼熱的天氣在這一地區還從來沒有過。）
- After so many years, she was still clinging to the hope that he could succeed.（許多年過去了，她仍抱著他會成功的希望。）

❷ The first is Ford (which brought it to a mass market), and the second Toyota [that has become a benchmark of quality and reliability (that all car manufacturers try to emulate)].

👉 **解析**

❶ …and the second Toyota that…second 和 Toyota 之間有一個 is 省略掉了。

❷ mark 是「痕跡、計號」，當動詞用是「標示、做計號」。老師批改學生考卷、作業時，會把錯誤、重要的地方 mark 起來，因此引申出「打成績、批分數」的意思；有時老師還會寫上 remark「評語、註解」，提醒學生注意事項。假如被標上特別的 mark，要想不 remarkable「顯著的、引人注目的」也難了。

benchmark 的 bench 並非「長板凳」，而是「工作台」。最早 benchmark 是指土地測量員在測量前先在岩壁上切出一個 mark，搭出一個簡易的 bench，然後把儀器擺在上面進行測量。這個 benchmark 便成為測量相對距離前必須先決定的參考點，進而衍生為「基準」。hallmark 原先指倫敦 Goldsmiths' Hall 礦石檢驗局在證實金銀純度的官方文件上所蓋的正字標計戳印。凡是文件蓋上這個 mark，就意味送檢的東西已經具備應有的「特徵、特點」了。

# The Innovators (2)

## Unit 2-4

## 創新者（2）

💡 閱讀原文：試用 **3** 分鐘的時間念完文章，記得先把中文遮上，並翻頁看題目問什麼。計時開始！

### The Innovators (2)

After a tour of British and American car factories, Kiichiro Toyoda became determined to produce world-class vehicles in Japan. (A) He carried out some **reverse** engineering on American car engines and at the end of the 1930s launched the Toyota car company. (B) Shortly after Toyoda retired from the company, his long standing **deputy** Eiji took over the **reins**.

Eiji and another **colleague** Ohno came up with the kanban system of labeling, a tool that allowed one to process to pull or acquire from the **proceeding** process only what was needed, when it was needed, and in the amount needed. Toyota introduced and followed kaizen, the philosophy of continuous improvement and cost cutting, which has helped to make Toyota the byword for quality and value for money it is today. (C) In recent years, JIT and the Toyota way of doing things have become widely accepted not just in the motor industry but elsewhere too. (D)

## 創新者（2）

　　英美汽車廠之旅以後，豐田喜一郎決心要在日本生產世界級的汽車。(A) 他對美國引擎進行逆向工程，在 1930 年代末期開創了豐田汽車公司。(B) 豐田喜一郎退休不久，長期以來的副手豐田英二隨即接掌大權。

　　豐田英二與同事大野耐一提出標籤看板管理系統，這種工具可以從生產過程中得知需要什麼、什麼時候需要、所需要的數量，進而拉動生產流程。豐田公司引進了「改善」的理念並奉行不渝，這是一套持續改進與節省成本的思想，它讓豐田打造出今天所象徵的品質、價值金字招牌。(C) 最近幾年，即時管理系統和豐田的處事風格不只在汽車界也在其他領域廣為接受肯定。(D)

## 考題演練及解析

Look at the four letters that indicate where the following sentence could be added to the passage.

**He pioneered the "just in time" production system, which took its name from the idea of replenishing material buffers, not before or after, but just when they were needed.**

Where could the sentence best fit?

看看文章裡四個字母，哪個地方可以把下面句子安插進去

他倡導「即時」生產系統，也就是不是之前，也不是之後，而是正當需要緩衝物料時，才進行補充，所謂「即時」便是因此而得名。

這句子放哪裡最合適？

### 解析

答案｜(B)

❶ 插入句題型假如題目出現 it、he、one 之類的代名詞或者 this、those、such 之類的指示詞，都是最佳解題線索，絕對不容輕易錯過。

❷ 看到題目開頭第一個字是代名詞 He，可以先心裡暗爽，因為只要順藤摸瓜把文章中 He 的藏鏡人找出來，答案便呼之欲出了。當然囉，藏鏡人絕對不能找錯！

❸ 題目主詞是 he，最至少前文一定會出現某一個男人，而且不至於離得太遠，因為代名詞離所代替的名詞當然愈近愈好。基於這一點，可以先排除 (C) (D) 選項，因為緊接 (C) 前面那一句主詞是 Toyota，不像答案。而 (D) 就離譜了，連考慮都免了。

❹ 剩下 (A) 和 (B) 都有可能。緊接 (A) 前面那一句主詞是 Kiichiro Toyoda，雖然有可能是答案，可是看看後文會發現當時豐田喜一郎才剛決心涉足汽車界，連公司都還沒創立，可是題目卻提到他倡導即時系統，邏輯不通。只有 (B) 毫無破綻。

*et* 1

*et* 2

從拆解商學、行銷類題目，看連接詞的角色 2

*et* 3

*et* 4

*et* 5

*et* 6

## ⚙ 深度應用分析：對付閱讀就是要化「繁」為「簡」。先刪去( )、[ ] 內的文字，找出主要的主詞和動詞！

❶ He pioneered the "just in time" production system, (which took its name from the idea of replenishing material buffers, not before or after, but just when they were needed.)

### 👉 解析

❶ 關係代名詞 which 引領子句說明先行詞 the "just in time" production system。重點是後面 not…but…對等連接詞「不是……而是……」，當中 not 後面再出現另一個對等連接詞 or。應該注意的是 or 處於正常肯定狀態時，意思是「兩者任一」，但是 or 要是跟 not 一起出現時，是意味「全部否定」。簡而言之，not…or… = neither…nor…「既不是……也不是……」。例如：The monk has no aspiration for fame or gain.（這位師父既不圖名，也不圖利。）

❷ bang、bump、buff 都是擬聲字，也就是物體撞擊產生的低沉聲音，之後也都帶有「撞擊、打擊」之意。後來汽車前面出現 bumper「保險桿」，可想而知目的就是萬一發生車禍時，bumper 會先承受撞擊，緩解汽車本體與駕駛人所受的

傷害。火車頭尾與軌道末端也有 buffer「緩衝器」，作用跟汽車的 bumper 一樣。material buffer「緩衝物料」說白一點就是「原料庫存量」

❷ Toyota introduced and followed kaizen, [(the philosophy of continuous improvement and cost cutting,) which has helped to make Toyota the byword for quality and value for money (it is today)].

👉 解析

❶ 這句話 kaizen 後面的小括號是它的同位語，說明 kaizen 是什麼概念；更後面的 which 關係代名詞帶領子句修飾先行詞 kaizen，告訴讀者 kaizen 所發揮的成效。

❷ 本文出現幾個日本字彙，其漢字發音就跟中文雷同，應該都猜得出來：kaizen 即カイゼン「改善」；kanban 即かんばん「看板」；最後一句的 JIT 就是題目那句話"just in time"「即時生產系統」的縮寫。

❸ 所謂 **byword** 就是 words to live by「座右銘」，引申即「典範」。

# Hunch or Reason? (1)

## 直覺或理性（1）

💡 閱讀原文：試用 **3** 分鐘的時間念完文章，記得先把中文遮上，並翻頁看題目問什麼。計時開始！

### Hunch or Reason? (1)

Some years ago the Getty museum in Malibu was offered an ancient Greek statue. When most art experts viewed it, they instinctively felt that it was a forgery. Scientific **analysis**, however, suggested it was **genuine** so Getty went ahead and bought it. Nevertheless, the jury is still out, for the statue carries the label 'Greek 530 B.C. or a modern forgery'! Getty had chosen factual analysis over instinctive hunch. On a hunch based on decades of living and breathing ancient art, the art expert could 'think without thinking' and, therefore, gave the statue the thumbs down.

Companies are not really supposed to make choices based on hunch or instinct. A manager buying a **fleet** of

**vans** for its delivery service will be expected to support a decision with hard facts about cost, fuel consumption, reliability, service packages, and carbon footprint. Similarly, huge capital project decisions cannot be taken lightly and have to be as **rational** and scientifically based as possible. Engineers and experts will estimate the challenges, costs, and **timescale** of a project before it is given the green light.

## 直覺或理性（1）

　　幾年前，有個古希臘雕像要賣給馬里布的蓋蒂博物館。大多數藝術行家看到時，都直覺認為是膺品。然而科學分析卻顯示是真品，所以蓋蒂博物館就批准買下來了。儘管如此，這事至今還尚未蓋棺論定，因為雕像上面還是標示著「西元前 530 年希臘或現代仿冒品」！蓋蒂博物館選擇的是事實分析，而非本能直覺。這些藝術行家幾十年來跟著古典藝術一起生活、一起呼吸，靠著這樣建立起來的直覺，就能想都不想，否決掉那個雕像。

　　公司實在不應該根據直覺或本能來做出抉擇。要買下一整隊廂型車來送貨的經理，於理應該要根據售價、耗油量、可靠度、全套服務、碳足跡這些鐵錚錚的事實而支持某一個決策。同理，動用龐大資金的專案下決策時絕不能掉以輕心，必須儘可能理性、講究科學。在給予綠燈放行之前，工程師、專家要針對挑戰、成本、企劃時間表作出評估。

Ch 1
Ch 2
從拆解商學、行銷類題目，看連接詞的角色 2
Ch 3
Ch 4
Ch 5
Ch 6

**Which of the following best expresses the essential information in the underlined sentence? Incorrect answer choices change the meaning in important ways or leave out essential information.**

(A) Because the statue turned out to be an illegal copy, the case went to court finally.

(B) The court comes to the judgment that the statue can date from 530 B.C., but the author does not believe it.

(C) It remains unclear whether the statue is genuine or not.

(D) Though the jury has arrived at its verdict that the statue is a counterfeit, it is actually not.

以下哪一句最能表達出劃底線句子的基本訊息？不正確的答案選項會以重要方式改變句義，或者遺漏基本訊息

(A) 因為這雕像到頭來竟然是非法複製品，所以這案子最後對簿公堂。

(B) 法院做出的裁決是這雕像可以追溯到西元前 350 年，可是本文作者卻不相信。

(C) 這雕像究竟是真是假仍舊懸而未決。

(D) 雖然陪審團裁定這雕像是冒牌貨，可是事實上它並不是。

### 解析

答案｜**(C)**

❶ 這一題核心就在 the jury is still out。jury 是「陪審團」，按照英美國家的審判程序，被告是否有罪由陪審團裁定。庭審結束後，陪審員離席，進入陪審室討論被告是否有罪以及如何定罪。在陪審員沒有回到法庭之前，審判結果當然無從得知。例如：The jury is still out on whether the jerrybuilt houses will be torn down.（那些偷工減料的房子是否要拆除目前還是一個大問號。）。得悉背後的典故，答案昭然若揭即 (C)。就算不知道這典故，後面的 or 還是洩漏了天機，因為 or 本身就暗示著不確定，這意味這雕像真假難辨。

❷ (C) 選項的 **genuine** 跟 **gene**「基因」同源。如果具有某種 gene，就意味這是與生俱來，不是人為假冒，當然是「真實的」。同理，所謂 **genius**「天才」就意味其才能是天生，並非後天栽培的 **ingenuous**，其字形、字義跟 genuine 比較像，意思是「天真的、坦率的」；**ingenious** 字形、字義跟 genius 比較像，意思是「聰明的、精巧的」。兩個字的字首 in- 都是 in 的意思，也就是 in the genes 來自基因的遺傳。

❶ Nevertheless, (the jury is still out), for (the statue carries the label 'Greek 530 B.C. or a modern forgery'!)

### 👉 解析

❶ for 當連接詞時，用法上和 because 最大的差異是，不能用於句首，例如：He had a great desire to have a home of his own, for he had always lived with my aunt.（他強烈渴望擁有一個屬於自己的家，因為他一直和我姑媽住在一起。）

❷ because、as、since 都是「因為」，可是三者還是有差異。根據 English Grammar Today 的說法，because 最常用，強調的是「因」；as 和 since 比 because 還正式，強調的是「果」。例如：

- As it's getting dark, let's stop working.（因為快天黑了，我們收工吧。）[ 強調收工這個結果 ]
- Because the weather was too terrible, they didn't enjoy the trip.（因為天氣太差，他們這趟旅遊並沒有玩得盡興。）[ 強調天氣不佳這個原因 ]

❷ A manager (buying a fleet of vans for its delivery service) will be expected to support a decision [with hard facts (about cost, fuel consumption, reliability, service packages, and carbon footprint.)]

### 👉 解析

❶ buying 帶領的分詞片語修飾前面的 a manager，也就是說經理正規劃花不少錢買車。will be expected 表示，根據一般人預料，這位經理應該要這樣做。介系詞片語 with hard facts 修飾動詞 support，表示拿出確切的事實來支持某個決定。哪些事實呢？就是列在 about 後面那五個因素 cost、fuel consumption、reliability、service packages、carbon footprint。

❷ 做決定最令人一個頭兩個大的就是在要和不要之間取捨；用英文表達「是否」時，到底是用 whether 還是 if 也是讓人霧沙沙。whether 畢竟比 if 來得正統，因此很多場合都只能用 whether，不能用 if。

例：

I want to know if he will attend the meeting.

He worried about whether he had hurt her feelings.

從拆解商學、行銷類題目，看連接詞的角色 2

# Hunch or Reason? (2)

## 直覺或理性（2）

 閱讀原文：試用 3 分鐘的時間念完文章，記得先把中文遮上，並翻頁看題目問什麼。計時開始！

### Hunch or Reason? (2)

But is factual analysis always the best way of arriving at the best business decisions? Managers need to do things right but leaders have to do the right thing. These people have to make difficult **strategic** decisions about how to take their companies forward. They have to **envisage** a future that may be unsupported by the facts that are available today. Careful research and analysis before you act doesn't always provide the answers.

And in our private lives, while we know we should make decisions about where we live and what we buy, decisions that can often involve large **sums** of money, on purely rational **criteria**, our instinct tells us what is right for us. (A) A poor decision will only affect ourselves. (B) If we trust experts, then it can help us avoid the blame if something goes wrong. (C) Sticking our necks out and trusting our instincts can have unhappy **consequences** if we are proved wrong. We are the perfect scapegoat. (D)

## 直覺或理性（2）

可是事實分析肯定是做出最棒的商業決策最棒的方法嗎？身為經理必須正確的做事，但是身為領導卻必須做出正確的事。這些人必須針對怎麼帶領公司前進，做出很困難的戰略決策。他們必須預見到一個今天還得不到事實證實的未來。就算行動前小心研究分析過，也不見得會求得答案。

在個人生活中，針對要住哪裡、買什麼，這些經常會牽涉到大筆金錢的決定，以純理性標準來做這種決定時，本能會告訴我們什麼對我們最適合。(A) 一個很糟糕的決定只會影響我們自己而已。(B) 假如相信專家，萬一出了差錯，就能避免我們受到指責。(C) 伸出脖子跟著直覺走，萬一證明自己錯了，這時結果就很不妙了，我們會成為最佳的替罪羔羊。(D)

## 考題演練及解析

Look at the four letters that indicate where the following sentence could be added to the passage.

**At work, whether we should always trust experts or our instincts is a more difficult question to answer.**

Where could the sentence best fit?

看看文章裡四個字母，哪個地方可以把下面句子安插進去

工作上，到底應該要相信專家還是直覺，是一個更難回答的問題。

這句子放哪裡最合適？

### 解析

答案｜(B)

❶ 解插入題型時，要先看看題目有沒有提供線索

一、有沒有代名詞、指示詞，有的話最好，只要找出幕後本尊，很快就可以迎刃而解。

二、有沒有轉折語，例如：

● 假如有 however、in spite of，就意味文章內容出現轉折，因此題目前一句內容可能會和題目相反。

● 假如有 therefore、consequently，就意味有因果關係，因此題目前一句內容可能就是講述原因。

- 假如有 moreover、besides，就意味題目的邏輯思維和前一句大致會差不多。

三、看看題目跟文章有沒有相對應的片語、單字。

四、萬一上述線索一個也沒有，那就只能靠硬功夫，單憑上下文邏輯去推測了。

❷ 本題屬於上面第三種狀況。題目一開頭是 At work…，正好對應文章第一句話 And in our private lives…顯然在比較個人人生活中與工作中做抉擇時，是要相信直覺還是理性？如果把答案放進 (A)，但是隨後的 A poor decision will only affect ourselves 則說明自己的決定僅會影響自己，無法和 At work 做連結。儘管如此，再放進 (B) 顯然就合理多了。

❶ At work, (whether we should always trust the experts or our instincts) is a more difficult question to answer.

### 📖 解析

❶ 連接詞 whether…or...的子句放在句首作主詞，這時不能用 if 代替 whether，但是可以用 it 做虛主詞，所以這句話也可以改成：

At work, it is a more difficult question to answer whether we should always trust the experts or our instincts.

❷ 整篇文章一直圍繞著該相信專家還是直覺這主題。從這一段之前所述都只是個人的決定，金額再怎麼大，頂多就是自己搞得灰頭土臉。後兩句緊接著又點出，這問題換到工作中，就得考慮到來自同事排山倒海的壓力。聽信專家的話，萬一出差錯，起碼有個保護傘；但是相信直覺，萬一出差錯，那就得成為 scapegoat 背黑鍋了。

❷ And in our private lives, while we know we should make decisions [about (where we live) and (what we buy)], [decisions (that can often involve large sums of money)], on purely rational criteria, our instinct tells us what is right for us.

### 解析

❶ …we should make decisions about 中的 about 介系詞片語修飾第一個 decisions，說明這是關於 where we live 和 what we buy 的決定。之後第二個 decisions 片語則是先前第一個 decisions 的同位語，說明這決定會牽涉到大筆金錢。

❷ 這句話的主要子句是最後面但是結構也最單純的 our instinct tells us what is right for us。跟在連接詞 while 後面的就是附屬子句 we know we should make decisions，這部分結構就變複雜的了，千萬不要看得眼花撩亂。首先往下的介系詞片語 about where we live and what we buy 是要修飾附屬子句的受詞 decisions。後面緊接上來的 decisions that can often involve large sums of money 是附屬子句的受詞 decisions 的同位語。值得注意的是介系詞片語 on purely rational criteria 是要當副詞修飾附屬子句 we should make decisions 的 make decisions，亦即以純理性標準來做這種決定。

# The Ultimate Delivery System (1)

## 終極快遞系統（1）

閱讀原文：試用 3 分鐘的時間念完文章，記得先把中文遮上，並翻頁看題目問什麼。計時開始！

### The Ultimate Delivery System (1)

Every day in **chaotic** Mumbai, a **logistical** miracle takes place. Teams of men wearing white hats deliver countless home-cooked lunches to office workers in the city. The lunch is contained in **aluminum** buckets called 'dabbas', and the men who deliver them are known as dabbawalas. What is amazing is that each dabba changes hands at least three times on its way. The system originated because there are so many different **ethnic** groups and **castes**, each with its own specific dietary needs and preferences. People would rather have a hot midday meal sent from their homes directly to their offices than find a restaurant. It is also up to fifteen times cheaper than eating out.

Without computers or mobile phones, the dabbawalas, mostly illiterate, deliver thousands of dabbas to their clients without fail, using a system of color-coding and signs. The network is so efficient that the business magazine, Forbes, gave it a six sigma performance rating, making it as reliable as Motorola or General Electric, despite the fact that a team of Harvard statisticians said it was **virtually** impossible.

## 終極快遞系統（1）

每天在混亂的孟買都會發生一件運輸補給的大奇蹟。好幾隊戴著白帽的男人把數不清自家烹煮的午餐轉送到城裡白領上班族手上。這頓午餐用一種叫「dabba」的鋁製桶子裝著，運送 dabba 的人便以 dabbawala 這稱呼為世人所知。最令人吃驚的是，運送途中每個 dabba 至少要轉三次手。這套系統的緣起於有這麼多不同的族群與種性階級，每一種都有自己特殊的飲食需求與喜好。老百姓寧願吃從自己家裡送過來熱騰騰的午餐，也不要上館子。這樣也比吃外食還便宜十五倍。

既沒電腦也沒手機，這些 dabbawala 大部分都是文盲，使用一種彩色編碼符號系統，將成千上萬個 dabba 送到客戶手中，使命必達。這套運輸網效率好到連富比士商業雜誌都給它六標準差的效能評比，簡直跟摩托羅拉、通用電氣一樣的可靠，儘管有一組哈佛統計學家說事實上這根本不可能。

**Which of the following best expresses the essential information in the underlined sentence? Incorrect answer choices change the meaning in important ways or leave out essential information.**

(A) In Mumbai, most office workers prefer eating home-cooked food in their workplace to eating out.

(B) Most people eat a proper, home-prepared meal for lunch more often than eat in a restaurant.

(C) Mumbaikars don't like to look for a clean restaurant any more than to enjoy the freshly-prepared food sent from their homes.

(D) People don't even bother to have the home-packed lunch; instead, they go to a restaurant.

以下哪一句最能表達出劃底線句子的基本訊息？不正確的答案選項會以重要方式改變句義，或者遺漏基本訊息

(A) 在孟買，大部分白領上班族都比較喜歡在工作場所吃自家食物，而非吃館子。

(B) 比起去餐廳吃飯而言，大部分人午餐更常常吃自家準備的餐點。

(C) 宛如不喜歡享用自己家裡送來的新鮮食物一樣，孟買人也不喜歡去找一家乾淨的餐廳。

(D) 人們甚至連自家午餐都懶得吃；相反的，他們去餐廳。

👉 **解析**

答案｜(A)

❶ 題目這句話用連接詞 than 連接兩個選項，表示孟買的老百姓比較喜歡吃自家便當，而不是吃食。即使不懂這句型，因為全文幾乎都是在談 dabba 便當和 dabbawala 便當快遞業者，一定是孟買百姓基於 ethnic「種族」、caste「社會階級」、價錢多方面的考量寧願吃自家便當，才讓這些便當快遞業者有混口飯吃的工作機會。因此答案肯定是指孟買人拒吃外食、喜歡吃自家伙食的習性。

❷ (A) 選項只是用 prefer…to…取代 would rather…than…其餘內容都不變，所以 (A) 是答案。

❸ (B) 選項把題意改成 more often，很明顯錯誤。(C) 選項 no more…than…這種句型乍看之下是比較級，實際上意味兩個都不喜歡。例如：She is no more stupid than you are. （她和你一樣不傻。）

❹ (D) 選項的 not bother 接不定詞意思是「連……嫌麻煩」。例如：
He didn't even bother to say thank you. （他甚至連說一聲謝謝都嫌麻煩。）

❶ People would rather [have a hot midday meal (sent from their homes directly to their offices)] than (find a restaurant).

**解析**

❶ would rather…than…句型意思是「寧願……也不願……」。受到助動詞 would 的影響，所以不只 rather 後面的動詞要原形，連接詞 than 後面的動詞也要原形。例如：

He would rather fail than cheat in the examination.

= He prefers to fail rather than cheat in the examination.

= He prefers failing to cheating in the examination.

（他寧願考不及格，也不願意作弊。）

❷ 從這句話的前後文可以得知孟買人喜歡吃自家便當的原因。從前面那句…there are so many different ethnic groups and castes…可以知道兩個原因，一個是種族複雜，一個是社會階級，導致各有各的飲食習慣，有的吃素，有的不吃牛肉，五花八門，即使想上餐廳，也不見得找得到自己屬意的。從後面那句 It is also up to fifteen times cheaper than eating out 又能得知，另一個因素是價錢太貴了。正是種種客觀因素，導致孟買會多出便當快遞服務這一門行業。

❷ The network is so efficient that the business magazine, Forbes, gave it a six sigma performance rating, (making it as reliable as Motorola or General Electric), despite the fact [that a team of Harvard statisticians said (it was virtually impossible)].

👉 解析

❶ 主要子句是表結果的 so…that…句型。注意後面的 despite 雖然和 but 意思都是「雖然」，但是詞性卻是介系詞，所以後面是接名詞 the fact 當受詞，而非子句，跟 in spite of 用法完全一樣。而後再來一個 that 連接詞子句，說明這個 the fact 原來是指哈佛大學的專家們對便當快遞業者的傑出表現直呼不可能。

❷ 這句話之所以給孟買便當快遞業者這麼高的評價，其原因就在上一句。這些快遞業者多數都是 illiterate「文盲」，在現在科技付之闕如的情況下，靠著最原始的方法，正確無誤的將便當送達指定地點，風雨無阻、使命必達。難怪本文標題取為 The Ultimate Delivery System，而且開頭第一句話就把孟買便當快遞服務形容為 a logistical miracle「運輸補給大奇蹟」

ch 1

ch 2

從拆解商學、行銷類題目，看連接詞的角色 2

ch 3

ch 4

ch 5

ch 6

# The Ultimate Delivery System (2)

## 終極快遞系統（2）

💡 閱讀原文：試用 3 分鐘的時間念完文章，記得先把中文遮上，並翻頁看題目問什麼。計時開始！

### The Ultimate Delivery System (2)

Take the case of Mr. Rahman, an office worker, for example. His dabba has a black swastika, a yellow dot and a red slash. Elsewhere there is a white cross and black circle. The first symbols tell the dabbawalas the train station to go to, the line to take, and where to get off; the remaining ones indicate the district and the building and floor where they need to be delivered. At 10 a.m. the first dabbawala turns up to collect Mr. Rahman's dabba from his wife at home. The dabba sets off on its journey. By 12:30 Mr. Rahman is tucking into his lunch.

It is a hazardous occupation riding a bicycle with a huge tray of dabbas, or rushing across busy roads to get to an office building on the other side. During the **monsoon** season, dabbawalas have to **wade** through water to get to their customers. If a dabbawala is incapacitated, another one will take over the dabba delivery lest the dabbas should fail to arrive at their destination in time.

## 終極快遞系統（2）

　　就拿一位白領上班族拉曼先生為例。他的 dabba 上面有一個黑色卍字、一個黃色圓點、一條紅色斜線；其他地方還有一個白色十字、黑色圓圈。第一組符號告訴 dabbawala 去哪個火車站、哪裡排隊、哪裡下車；其餘那一組則指示要送到哪一區、哪一棟大樓的第幾樓。早上十點第一個 dabbawala 在拉曼先生家門口出現，從他老婆手中收到 dabba，這便當就展開它的行程。到 12:30 時，拉曼先生正埋首吃午餐了。

　　這行業要拿著裝著 dabba 的大托盤騎單車，或者闖越繁忙的街道到另一邊的辦公大樓，真是險象環生。雨季時，dabbawala 還必須涉水去找客戶。如果 dabbawala 有三長兩短，另一名會來接手，以免那個便當不能及時送達目的地。

**Which of the following statements about the dabbawala is supported by this passage?**

(A) The dabbawalas begin to work early in the morning.

(B) The dabbawalas must learn to recognize a unique but complicated abstract symbols so as to deliver each dabba to the right customer wherever in Mumbai that person is.

(C) After lunch, the dabbawalas collect the dabba from the desks they delivered to, and bring them back to the home where it started from.

(D) Should adabbawala have an accident, his coworker will cover his shift to ensure the dabba won't miss the deadline.

根據本文，以下關於 dabbawala 的陳述何者為真？

(A) dabbawala 一大早就開始工作

(B) dabbawala 必須學習辨識一套獨特卻複雜的抽象符號，以便把便當正確無誤地送到客人手上，不管那人在孟買哪個地方

(C) 午餐後，dabbawala 去客戶辦公室取回便當，然後把它們帶回客戶家裡，亦即原先最早的起點

(D) 萬一 dabbawala 發生意外，他的同事會代他的班，確保這

個便當不至於錯過時限。

## 🖐 解析

答案 | **(D)**

❶ 早上十點 dabbawala 才開始去客戶家裡拿便當，工作時間應該是 late in the morning，所以 **(A)** 不對。

❷ **(B)** 幾乎都正確，但是卻出現一顆老鼠屎，以至於整鍋粥全報銷了：complicated。從本文第二句話就知道一個便當前前後後就五個符號。十點時 the first dabbawala 來拿便當，注意那個 first，這意味這只是便當快遞接力中的第一棒而已，中間還要轉好幾手，每一位 dabba 接棒後只要會辨識專屬自己負責那一個符號就行了，這樣還不夠簡單嗎？幹這一行的大多數是文盲，假如這套編碼符號系統太複雜，豈不是三不五時就搞得天下大亂。因此這套系統 **abstract**「抽象」沒錯，但是並不 complicated「複雜」。

❸ 注意要看清題目。**(C)** 選項敘述可能沒錯，但是本文並沒有提到這件事，因此 **(C)** 還是不對。

❹ 注意 **(D)** 是假設法的倒裝句型，原來應該是 If a dabbawala should have an accident⋯，會用 should 意味發生機率不高。這選項正好反映出文章的最後一句，所以答案就是 **(D)**。

## 深度應用分析：對付閱讀就是要化「繁」為「簡」。先刪去( )、[] 內的文字，找出主要的主詞和動詞！

❶ If (a dabbawala is incapacitated), [(another one will take over the dabba delivery) lest (the dabbas should fail to arrive at their destination in time)].

### 解析

❶ 這句話有兩個連接詞 if 和 lest，lest 後面引導的子句常常會加上 should。這個 should 也可以省略，不過省略歸省略，後面的動詞還是要原形。例如：He brought an umbrella with him lest it (should) rain this afternoon.（他帶了傘，以免今天下午下雨。）

❷ lest = in case = for fear that，所以後面那句也可以寫成：…another one will take over the dabba delivery in case the dabbas fails to arrive at their destination in time.

❸ incapacitate = in(not) + capacit + ate(動詞字尾)
incapacitate 這個字雖然有點深度，但是從字形依然看得出來跟 capacity 很像。萬一很不幸還是不知道 capacity 是何方神聖，那麼應該認識它的形容詞 capable 了吧？是的，be

capable of 曝光率高多了，知名度雖然還比不上 be able to，但是也算是小有名氣；

形容詞　capable　　「能幹的、有能力的」

名詞　　capacity　　「才能、能力」

動詞　　capacitate　「使有能力」

capacitate　　加上表否定的字首 in-，incapacitate 當然是「失去能力」。

❷ The first symbols tell the Dabbawalas (the train station to go to), (the line to take), and (where to get off); the remaining ones indicate [the district and the building and floor (where they need to be delivered)].

### 👈 解析

❶ 這句話以分詞連接兩句，各自說明便當上兩組符號代表什麼意思。The first symbols 是指前面提到的 a black swastika、a yellow dot、a red slash 這些符號；remaining 後面的 ones 代替前面的 symbols，也就是 a white cross、black circle 這些符號。

❷ 之所以會需要這一套符號系統，無非是便當快遞業者很多都是 illiterate「文盲」。要讓所有文盲都看得懂，這套符號系統當然必須要簡單明瞭。

## Unit 3-1

# The Church and the State (1)

# 政治與宗教（1）

💡 閱讀原文：試用 3 分鐘的時間念完文章，記得先把中文遮上，並翻頁看題目問什麼。計時開始！

### The Church and the State (1)

(A) On the surface, the First Amendment to the Constitution seems simple and **unambiguous**. (B) It appears to **assert** quite clearly that one's religious faith is not and should not be interfered with by the government, and that the government should not support one religion over another. (C)

The earliest European settlers came to America seeking freedom to worship, particularly after the English Civil War and religious conflict in France and Germany. (D) They had little **forbearance**, however, when it came to allowing others the same freedom. In most of the early colonies, religion was considered part of government. Not only was there no freedom to practice a differing faith, but the **dominant** religion of the colony **encroached** on every facet of one's life. A man was not allowed to vote or hold office unless he was a member of the church. The governing bodies could **impose** taxes on all members of the community for the support of the church.

## 政治與宗教（1）

(A) 表面上，憲法第一條修正案似乎簡單明瞭，(B) 很明確地宣稱一個人的宗教信仰不可以而且不應該受到政府干涉，以及政府不應該偏袒任何一種宗教。(C)

最早的歐洲移民是來美洲尋求信仰自由，特別是在英國內戰與德、法宗教衝突之後。(D) 儘管如此，一談到允許別人也有同樣自由時，他們的包容心也沒好到哪裡去。大部分早期殖民地都把宗教視為政府的一部分。不只沒有不同信仰的自由，殖民地勢力最大的宗教甚至還侵犯到一個人生活中每個層面。除非是教會成員，否則一個人不准投票或從事公職。為了資助教會，管理團體可以對社區所有成員徵稅。

Look at the four letters that indicate where the following sentence could be added to the passage.

**Contrary to popular belief, however, this very principle that is commonly referred to as "the separation of church and state" does not appear in the Constitution.**

Where could the sentence best fit?

看看文章裡四個字母，哪個地方可以把下面句子安插進去

然而正好與大眾普遍的觀念相反，這條一般被稱呼為「政教分離」的原則，憲法裡並沒有出現。

這句子放哪裡最合適？

## 解析

答案｜(C)

❶ 從題目句子裡一開頭就出現 Contrary to popular belief 和 however，暗示語意會來個急轉彎。

❷ 緊接而來 this very principle 代表前面一定提過某個原則。

❸ 再往後又說明這個原則叫做「政教分離」，而且美國憲法對這麼重要的原則竟然隻字不提。回頭看本文第一句的 the

First Amendment to the Constitution 暗示美國憲法有漏洞，否則就沒必要再來個什麼 amendment。

❹ 根據以上線索，(A) (B) 兩個選項可以先排除。(C) 和 (D) 似乎差不多，但是 TOEFL 文章有如學術論文，每段開頭第一二句往往是闡明整段大意的主題句，而第二段內容主要是關於早期移民政教合一的淵源與狀況，已經跟憲法修正案無關了，因此 (D) 也不適當。把題目這一句安排在 (C) 這個位置顯然比較緊湊。

❺ 或許你不知道 amendment 是什麼，**mend** 有「修補、康復」的意思，所以 **amend** 是「修正、改進」，而 **amendment** 便是 **amend** 的名詞「修正案」。還有一個 **emend**「校訂、修改」。

## ⚙ 深度應用分析：對付閱讀就是要化「繁」為「簡」。先刪去( )、[ ]內的文字，找出主要的主詞和動詞！

❶ Contrary to popular belief, however, this very principle (that is commonly referred to as "the separation of church and state") does not appear in the Constitution.

**解析**

❶ 括號裡的 that 關係子句的先行詞是 this very principle。

本句的 very 沒有意思，作用是加強名詞的語氣，例如：

At that very moment the guest arrived.

（正好那時候客人來了。）

❷ 凡是先行詞符合以下條件，關係代名詞只能用 that，不能用 who 或 which

(1) 先行詞有 the only、the same、the very 修飾，例如：

He was the only person that knew how to open the safe.（他是唯一知道怎麼打開那保險櫃的人。）

(2) 先行詞有序數或最高級修飾，例如：

Neil Armstrong was the first man that walked on the moon.（阿姆斯壯是第一位在月球漫步的人。）

(3) 因為關係代名詞 who、which 正好也是疑問詞，所以在以疑問詞開頭的疑問句中，為避免重複混淆，關係代名詞應該儘量用 that，例如：Who is the man that has white hair?（那位白髮的人是誰？）

(4) 先行詞是人與非人，例如：

The car and the driver that fell into the river last night have not been found.（昨晚掉進河裡的汽車和司機還沒找到）

❷ It appears to assert quite clearly [(that one's religious faith is not and should not be interfered with by the government), and (that the government should not support one religion over another.)]

📢 解析

❶ 本句的 it 並非虛主詞，而是指前面那一句話的 the First Amendment to the Constitution。

❷ assert 後面有兩個 that 子句作受詞，也就是清楚的斷言兩個條件：政府不該干涉宗教，同樣不該偏袒任何一種宗教。其中第一個 that 可以省略，但是第二個 that 不能。

❸ 補充一下，假如先行詞是前面整個句子，關係代名詞就一定用 which，而且只能用補述用法，亦即前面要打個逗點。例如：It was raining, which kept him from coming, [which 就是指 It was raining 這件事]（正在下雨，他因而不能來。）

Unit 1

Unit 2

Unit 3

從拆解文化題目，看關係子句的角色

Unit 4

Unit 5

Unit 6

# Unit 3-2

## The Church and the State (2)

## 政治與宗教（2）

💡 閱讀原文：試用 3 分鐘的時間念完文章，記得先
把中文遮上，並翻頁看題目問什麼。計時開始！

### The Church and the State (2)

Given this history, one might wonder how the United States came to require the separation of church and state. Much happened between the arrival of the **Pilgrims** and the **drafting** of the Constitution more than 150 years later. What with the increase of population and what with better roads, people were less secluded. People of differing views might live close together; in addition, many later settlers came to make money rather than to practice their religious beliefs. By 1787 religion was no longer considered the government's concern.

Even so, just how separate church and state are is a source of **contention**. In 1962 the **Supreme** Court decided that school prayer violated the First Amendment. Similar challenges have been leveled against town-sponsored Christmas displays and the phrase "under God" in the **Pledge** of **Allegiance**. Not everyone, however, agrees with these decisions. The meaning of the phrase "separation of church and state" is far from settled.

## 政治與宗教（2）

　　有鑑於這一段歷史，一個人可能想知道美國是怎麼慢慢變成政教分離。在清教徒抵達和憲法起草這 150 多年之間發生了很多事。因為人口增加與道路改善，所以人們不再那麼疏離，不同想法的人可能會住在一塊。此外，許多後來的移民是為了賺錢而來，而非為了什麼宗教理念。到了 1787 年，宗教就不再被視為政府的重要考量。

　　政教要分離到什麼程度還是爭論的焦點。1962 年最高法院作出學校公禱違反第一條修正案的判決。鄉鎮贊助的聖誕節表演以及效忠宣誓裡的「在神護祐之下」這句話，都受到同樣的質疑。然而並不是每個人都贊同這些判決。「政教分離」的定義要喬攏還早得很。

Unit 1

Unit 2

Unit 3

從拆解文化題目，看關係子句的角色

Unit 4

Unit 5

Unit 6

**Which of the following best expresses the essential information in the underlined sentence? Incorrect answer choices change the meaning in important ways or leave out essential information.**

(A) More immigrants and a convenient traffic network made it easier for settlers to associate with different people.

(B) What people wanted was more neighbors and better roads in order that they would not be isolated from each other.

(C) With a view to attracting more residents and building better public transport facilities, colonists tried to interact with other people.

(D) Inhabitants could come into more social contact with others if more people settled in America and if traffic became better.

以下哪一句最能表達出劃底線句子的基本訊息？不正確的答案選項會以重要方式改變句義，或者遺漏基本訊息

(A) 更多人移入以及方便的交通網使得移民更容易和不同的人往來。

(B) 老百姓所要的就是更多鄰居和更好的道路，這樣彼此才不至於疏離。

(C) 為了吸引更多居民以及建立更好的交通設施，殖民者只好努力去跟其他人互動。

(D) 假如更多人在美國定居，交通變得更好，居民們就可以和其他人有更多社交接觸。

### 解析

答案｜(A)

❶ 句構重述題解題時，弄清整句的邏輯關係很重要，因為句子不管怎麼改，最根本的邏輯關係一定不容走樣。常見的邏輯關係有三種：轉折、因果、比較。假如題目有 because，答案可能改寫成 so、therefore；題目有 though，答案可能改成 but、however。然而考題不可能這麼制式規格化，改寫出來結果一定是千變萬化。譬如說用 cause、originate、result 來表達因果關係，這時就要練就一對提高警覺，從字裡行間抓出重要線索。

❷ 首先要注意題目這句子核心部分是 what with 表原因的慣用語，可是完了！四個選項竟然都沒有表達因果的字眼，顯然因果關係玩起了隱身術。

❸ (B) 的 what 和題目句的 what 雖然都是複合關係代名詞，但是實際意思上卻是風馬牛不相及。尤其是後面 in order that 是表目的，顯然語意誤入歧途了。(C) with a view to 也是表

目的，又來一個走偏的。(D) 變成 if 條件句，照樣失焦了。
答案 (A) 把因果關係藏在 make 虛受詞的句型裡。

## ⚙️ 深度應用分析：對付閱讀就是要化「繁」為「簡」。先刪去( )、[ ] 內的文字，找出主要的主詞和動詞！

❶ What with the increase of population and what with better roads, people were less secluded.

### 👉 解析

❶ what with A and (what with) B 是複合關係代名詞 what 的慣用語，意思「半因 A 半因 B」，表原因。類似的慣用語還有 what by A and (what by) B「半由 A 半由 B」，表方法。例如：What by bribes and what by extortion, he finally achieved his purpose.（半由賄賂，半由敲詐，他總算達成目的）

❷ 其實有些場合 with 本身就有「因為」的涵義，例如：
The girl blushed with embarrassment.
（這女孩因難為情而臉紅。）
His fingers were numb with cold.
（他的手指因冷而麻木了。）

❷ People of differing views might live close together; in addition, many later settlers came (to make money) rather than (to practice their religious beliefs).

### 👉 解析

❶ 兩個括號裡面的 to 都是表目的的 in order to，用 rather than 連接，表示後來的移民來到新大陸，目的是為了賺錢，而不是為了追求宗教信念。

❷ 本段大意是美國怎麼從政教合一走向政教分離。前一句話說因為人口增加和交通逐漸發達，老百姓互動慢慢熱絡起來。這一句進一步解釋不同見解的人混居在一塊，以及更多逐利而來的移民，逐漸把早期狂熱的清教徒愈稀釋愈淡薄，到了 1787 年美國獨立戰爭打得如火如荼時，政治和宗教已經徹底分家了。

❸ which 的所有格跟 who 所有格一樣都是 whose，但是因為也可以透過介系詞 of 來表達事物的所有狀態，所以 which 的所有格會有兩種呈現方式，茲舉一例：

The book whose cover is brown is mine.

= The book the cover of which is brown is mine.

= The book of which the cover is brown is mine

（封面是棕色的那本書是我的。）

### Unit 3-3

# The Arthurian Legend (1)

# 亞瑟王傳奇（1）

💡 閱讀原文：試用 3 分鐘的時間念完文章，記得先把中文遮上，並翻頁看題目問什麼。計時開始！

### The Arthurian Legend (1)

What mental images do you get when you think of King Arthur and the Knights of the Round Table? For most people, the mention of King Arthur evokes pictures of **virtuous** knights in polished armor riding **magnificent** horses in search of adventure. However, there is no firm evidence that King Arthur ever really existed.

This **nebulous** history has provoked an enormous number of Arthurian legends. It allowed generations of anonymous storytellers to enlarge on what few "facts" were known about this defender of their island. Audiences readily accepted these yarns of a native hero and added to them as they were passed along.

Like some of our own stories about George Washington, the stories gave Arthur all the qualities that the society held in high **esteem**. Consequently, King Arthur is **portrayed** as possessing the **chivalrous** qualities of the Middle Ages – bravery, courtesy, honor, and gallantry toward women. Also, since Arthur fought against heathen invaders, the stories took on a religious aspect. The broad assortment of stories about King Arthur are a mixture of history, legend, fairy tale, and moral lesson.

## 亞瑟王傳奇（1）

一想到亞瑟王與圓桌武士，你心裡會浮現什麼影像？對大部分人來說，一談到亞瑟王，總是喚起這樣的影像：品行端正的武士穿著晶亮的甲冑，騎著雄壯的駿馬四處去冒險。然而根本沒有亞瑟王存在過的確切證據。

這段朦朧的歷史引爆了多如繁星的亞瑟王傳奇，讓一代又一代不知名的說書人把這位島嶼守護者一星半點的「真相」渲染下去。觀眾對這位本土英雄的也十分買單，在代代傳承的過程中又為它們添油加醋。就像我們某些關於喬治華盛頓的故事一樣，這些故事也賦予了亞瑟所有社會中高度推崇的人格，結果就把亞瑟王描述成擁有中古世紀騎士特質——勇敢、謙恭、榮耀、對女性殷勤。此外，因為亞瑟抗擊異教侵略者，這些故事也染上了宗教色彩。關於亞瑟王五花八門的故事可說是揉合了歷史、傳說、童話、道德教育。

**Which of the following best expresses the essential information in the underlined sentence? Incorrect answer choices change the meaning in important ways or leave out essential information.**

(A) Originally there was only scanty information about King Arthur, but more and more truth was found through the efforts of innumerable nameless authors.

(B) Though little was known about King Arthur, countless unknown writers continued to embellish the legends with more and more details.

(C) Historical facts made more and more Englishmen believe King Arthur to be the protector of their country.

(D) Generations after generations of unrecognized narrators pieced together the truth about King Arthur from very few sketchy accounts.

以下哪一句最能表達出劃底線句子的基本訊息？不正確的答案選項會以重要方式改變句義，或者遺漏基本訊息

(A) 本來關於亞瑟王的資訊才一點點而已，但是透過數不清無名作家的努力，終於發現愈來愈多真相

(B) 雖然對亞瑟王的了解並不多，但是無數不為人知的作家持續不斷為這些傳説添血加肉。

(C) 歷史真相讓愈來愈多英國人相信亞瑟王就是他們國家的守護者。

(D) 一代又一代的無名說書人從寥如晨星的敘述中，拼湊出亞瑟王的真相。

## 解析

答案｜(B)

❶ 畫底線句開頭 it 是指前一句的 This nebulous history。第一段結尾就已經說明亞瑟王傳說其實是虛構的，前一句還用 nebulou「朦朧的」，而這句的 fact 又特地用引號標示，提醒讀者這些 fact 的可信度應該打個大問號。

❷ few、little 只要前面沒有 a，都意味少得接近零，這一句也不例外。尤其是前面 generations of anonymous storytellers 世世代代說書人為數不少，動詞又用 enlarge，意味原先少得可憐的亞瑟王傳說在不斷渲染下，像滾雪球一樣愈滾愈大，但是一樣毫無真實性可言。

❸ 把握住亞瑟王傳說真實性接近零的原則來判斷答案，當然就談不上什麼 truth、fact 這些字眼。(A) 說 more and more truth，顯然差得多；(C) 選項開門見山 Historical facts 也行不通； (D) 選項再度提到 truth，同樣不行。(B) 選項提到亞瑟王用的字是 legend，自始至終完全和 truth、fact 保持距離，即正確答案。

### ⚙️ 深度應用分析：對付閱讀就是要化「繁」為「簡」。先刪去( )、[ ] 內的文字，找出主要的主詞和動詞！

**❶** It allowed generations of anonymous storytellers to enlarge on what few "facts" were known about this defender of their island.

### 👉 解析

**❶** 這句話的 what 文法上叫做「關係形容詞」，跟關係詞一樣，兼具形容詞與連接詞的作用。例如：

You may take whichever book you like.

（你喜歡哪本書都可以拿走）

關係形容詞 what 和名詞之間可以放 little、few，其含意為「雖然少，還是把所有的…」，本句就是如此，亦即亞瑟王的史料原本就寥寥可數，但是說書人還是就那一點東西火力全開發揮得淋漓盡致。例如：

I gave my father what little money I had.

（我把所有的一點錢都給了我爸爸）

**❷** anonymous= ano(without) + nym(name) + ous(形容詞字尾)「匿名的、不具名的」。字根 nym、nomin 其實就是 name、noun「名詞」。

❷ For most people, the mention of King Arthur evokes pictures of virtuous knights (in polished armor)(riding magnificent horses)(in search of adventure).

👉 解析

❶ 括號裡面的介系詞片語 in polished armor、分詞片語 riding magnificent horses、介系詞片語 in search of adventure 都是要修飾前面的 knights。

❷ as 是準關係代名詞，that 可以做關係代名詞，兩個字正巧都可以和 such、the same 連用，但是所代表的涵義卻不同。例：

● This is the same bicycle that he bought.

（這就是他買的那部腳踏車。）因為先行詞是 the same bicycle，所以關係代名詞只能用 that，不能改用 which。

● This is the same bicycle as he bought.

（這部腳踏車跟他買的那部同款式。）這個 as 是準關係代名詞，先行詞也是 the same bicycle。

● He is such an honest man that we respect him.

（他這人這麼誠實，以至於我們都尊敬他。）這是 such… that… 表結果的句型；這個 that 是連接詞。

● He is such an honest man as we respect.

（他就跟我們所尊敬的那種誠實人一樣。）這個 as 是準關係代名詞，先行詞是 such an honest man。

# The Arthurian Legend (2)

# 亞瑟王傳奇（2）

 閱讀原文：試用 3 分鐘的時間念完文章，記得先把中文遮上，並翻頁看題目問什麼。計時開始！

### The Arthurian Legend (2)

According to the legend, Arthur was the son of King Uther Pendragon, but he was raised by Merlin the magician and Sir Hector. Arthur proved his claim to the **throne** by pulling a sword, the magic Excalibur, from a great stone, something no one else could do. He married Guinevere, whose father gave him as a dowry the Round Table, which, as its name suggests, had no head, implying that everyone who sat there had equal status. Conflict arose in this peaceful kingdom when Arthur's nephew, Mordred, **hatched** a **sinister plot** to overthrow Arthur. Mordred was slain in the **ensuing** battle, and Arthur was mortally wounded. His body was taken to an island where he supposedly would be healed and return to continue his reign.

Narrative poems, great operas, and even Broadway musicals have been based on the Arthurian legend. Few people really care whether a King Arthur truly existed. The stories are alive.

## 亞瑟王傳奇（2）

根據傳說，亞瑟是尤瑟·潘德拉剛國王的兒子，但是卻由梅林魔法師和赫克特爵士撫養成人。亞瑟從一塊大石頭中拔出一把寶劍，也就是神奇的王者之劍，這是其他人根本做不來的事，從而登基為王。他跟桂妮薇結婚，岳父送他一張圓桌當嫁妝。顧名思義，這桌子沒有頭尾，意味任何坐在那裏的每一個人地位都完全平等。當亞瑟的外甥莫德雷德策劃了一個要推翻亞瑟的邪惡陰謀時，在這寧靜的王國點燃了衝突的火種。莫德雷德在之後的戰役中被殺斃命，亞瑟王也得了致命傷。他的屍體被帶到一個小島，據說在那裡他會痊癒，然後回來繼續統治下去。

敘述詩、大型歌劇、甚至是百老匯音樂劇都改編自亞瑟王傳說。幾乎沒有人會在乎亞瑟王是否真正存在過。這些故事萬古流芳。

**Based on this passage, which of the following is FALSE?**

(A) Because Arthur drew Excalibur out of a stone, he was crowned king.

(B) The Round Table was built to ensure Arthur could chair a meeting so that all other knights were considered equal.

(C) The final battle claimed the lives of both Mordred and Arthur.

(D) The Round Table was a wedding gift from Arthur's father-in-law.

根據這篇文章，以下哪一個是錯誤的？

(A) 因為亞瑟王從石頭中拔出王者之劍，所以登基為王。

(B) 圓桌特地做成讓亞瑟可以主持會議，這樣所有其他武士就一律平等了。

(C) 最後的決戰中，莫德雷德和亞瑟都喪生了。

(D) 圓桌是亞瑟岳父送的結婚禮物。

👉 **解析**

答案｜**(B)**

❶ (A) 選項就是第二句 Arthur proved his claim to the throne by pulling a sword, the magic Excalibur,…，the magic Excalibur 是 a sword 的同位語，亦即那把劍名字叫做 Excalibur。

❷ (C) 選項則是第一段倒數第二句 Mordred was slain in the ensuing battle, and Arthur was mortally wounded。slay「殘殺」跟 slaughter「屠宰」同源。mortal「致命的」跟 mortuary「喪葬的、太平間」同源。Mordred 被 slay 當然是掛了，但是亞瑟王 mortally wounded 一樣難逃一死，所以 (C) 敘述正確。

❸ (B) (D) 選項都是第三句。

(D) 是…Guinevere whose father gave him as a dowry the Round Table…這部分。Guinevere 的爸爸當然是亞瑟王的丈人；dowry「嫁妝」說簡單一點就是 wedding gift。

(B) 是句尾…everyone who sat there had equal status。注意圓桌之所以設計成圓形，是希望所有同席人員不分主從每一個都平起平坐，但是(B)選項說亞瑟王 chair a meeting。chair 當動詞用時，意思是當 chairperson「主席」，這樣豈不是亞瑟王地位凌駕眾人之上？因此答案就是 (B)。

## ⚙ 深度應用分析：對付閱讀就是要化「繁」為「簡」。先刪去( )、[ ] 內的文字，找出主要的主詞和動詞！

---

❶ He married Guinevere,{whose father gave him as a dowry the Round Table, (which, as its name suggests, had no head), [implying that everyone (who sat there) had equal status.]}

👉 **解析**

❶ 關係代名詞的所有格 whose 帶領整個大括號裡面的子句修飾 Guinevere。

❷ …whose father gave him as a dowry the Round Table…正常應該寫成

…whose father gave him the Round Tableas a dowry…但是因為 the Round Table 後面要修飾它的 which 關係子句很長，只好讓 as a dowry 往前移動。

❸ implying 分詞片語也是修飾 the Round Table，亦即 which 關係子句原本是以下兩個句子合併而成的分詞構句

(1) The Round Table, as its name suggests, had no head.

(2) The Round Table implied that everyone who sat there had equal status.

❷ His body was taken to an island (where he supposedly would be healed and return to continue his reign).

## 👉 解析

❶ 關係副詞 where 帶領子句修飾 island，這個 where 可以改成 on which。

❷ 關係副詞 where 帶領的子句也可以當作地方副詞，例如：

- He asked me to stay where I was.
  （他叫我在待在原地。）
- The ship is to boldly go where none has gone before.
  （這艘船將勇敢航向無人曾到之處。）
- 關係副詞 when 和 where 一樣，也有非限定的補述用法，注意這時候 when 意思並不是一般最常見的「當」，更不是「什麼時候」，而是「那時」，例如：Most students will sleep late on Sunday, when they don't have to go to school.（大部分學生星期天都會睡晚一點，那一天他們不必上學。）

❸ 關係副詞 = 介系詞 + 關係代名詞。假如把關係副詞子句前面的先行詞省略，這時關係副詞子句也可以當作名詞子句，像上述第 2 點三個例句都是名詞子句。

*Ch* 1

*Ch* 2

*Ch* 3

從拆解文化題目，看關係子句的角色

*Ch* 4

*Ch* 5

*Ch* 6

# Unit 3-5

# Icarus and Daedalus (1)

# 伊卡魯斯和泰達路斯（1）

閱讀原文：試用 3 分鐘的時間念完文章，記得先把中文遮上，並翻頁看題目問什麼。計時開始！

### Icarus and Daedalus (1)

King Minos was the son of Zeus, the most important of the Greek gods. Minos, who ruled the island of Crete, was a **fickle** tyrant. He might love his subjects one day and **despise** them the next. Daedalus and his son Icarus were the victims of the king's changeable moods. (A) Even though Daedalus had built the famous **Labyrinth** for King Minos, the king had Daedalus and his son imprisoned on an island. (B)

The seagulls, which Daedalus and Icarus spent their days watching float freely through the air, gave Daedalus an idea for escaping his unjust incarceration. (C) The feathers were tied together with string and poured with melted wax. As the wax cooled and hardened, it formed a **cohesive** glue. (D) Next Daedalus fastened the wings to his shoulders and began to **cleave** the air by flapping his new wings back and forth. Slowly he began to rise from the ground, and glide over his island prison.

## 伊卡魯斯和泰達路斯（1）

　　米諾斯王是希臘諸神中最重要的宙斯之子。統治著克里特島的米諾斯是喜怒無常的暴君，可能哪一天還把自己的臣民捧在手掌心，隔天就棄如敝屣。泰達路斯和兒子伊卡魯斯就是這位國王善變心情下的倒楣鬼。(A) 即使泰達路斯為米諾斯王蓋了有名的迷宮，還是跟兒子一起被囚禁在一個小島上。(B)

　　泰達路斯和伊卡魯斯成天看著海鷗自由的在空中飄浮飛翔，泰達路斯因此想出一個點子，要逃離這不公不義的監禁。(C) 他把羽毛用繩子捆住，再倒上融化的蠟。隨著蠟冷卻硬化，就變成黏膠。(D) 接下來泰達路斯把翅膀固定在肩膀上，翅膀來來回回振動撥開空氣，慢慢的從地面騰空而起，在囚禁他的島嶼上空滑翔。

eH 1

eH 2

eH 3

從拆解文化題目，看關係子句的角色

eH 4

eH 5

eH 6

## 考題演練及解析

Look at the four letters that indicate where the following sentence could be added to the passage.

**Daedalus began to collect feathers from which to make a pair of enormous wings.**

Where could the sentence best fit?

看看文章裡四個字母，哪個地方可以把下面句子安插進去

他開始收集羽毛做出一對巨大的翅膀。

這句子放哪裡最合適？

答案｜**(C)**

❶ 有的插入句題目有提供線索，有的沒有。所謂「線索」可以分成以下幾種：

(1) 代名詞或指示詞，例如 it、they、he、those、this。雖然只是替身而已，但是它們卻有助於找到真身，前提是考生自己的導引系統必須要很精準。

(2) 關鍵形容詞，例如 such、another、next、former…等。假如題目句是：

Water possesses another most unusual

characteristic.

有沒有注意到 another？another 不可能憑空而來，出現這個字意味前面一定有提到水的特性，後面也會提到。這句話肯定處於列舉水諸多特性的句子之中，不會是第一句，也不會是最後一句，但是有可能是主題句。

(3) 關鍵名詞。假如題目句是：

However, the research was unable to come up with a reason why women should be more affected by working irregular or extended hours.

本文的 the research 意味之前一定提過一項調查，內容應該會跟加班有關。

❷ 比較可惜的是，本句沒提供多少有用的線索。所幸本文是一篇希臘神話，凡是內容是敘述體裁，大致都會按時間先後順序平鋪直敘，一路看下去就知道答案是 (C)。

*ed* 1

*ed* 2

*ed* 3

從拆解文化題目，看關係子句的角色

*ed* 4

*ed* 5

*ed* 6

⚙ **深度應用分析：對付閱讀就是要化「繁」為「簡」。先刪去( )、[ ] 內的文字，找出主要的主詞和動詞！**

❶ Daedalus began to collect feathers from which to make a pair of enormous wings.

☞ **解析**

❶ 這句話由以下兩句構成

(1) Daedalus began to collect feathers

(2) Daedalus could make a pair of enormous wingsfrom these feathers.

這兩句可以合併成：

Daedalus began to collect feathers from which he could make a pair of enormous wings.

兩句主詞都是 Daedalus，為了精簡，省略掉其中一個 Daedalus，也就是合併後的 he。既然主詞不見了，就不再是子句，也沒必要再保留動詞，因此乾脆用不定詞取代動詞。這時關係子句就蛻變成為：介系詞 + 關係代名詞 + 不定詞。但是為什麼會冒出介系詞？當然是因為關係子句裡原來的動詞是不及物動詞。不及物動詞後面不能接受詞，如果有的話，應該先來一個介系詞，讓受詞成為介系詞的受詞才行。

❷ 茲再舉一例：

They have a big garden and they can play in the garden.

= They have a big garden in which they can play.

= They have a big garden in which to play.

= They have a big garden to play in.

❷ The seagulls, [which Daedalus and Icarus spent their days watching (float freely through the air)], gave Daedalus an idea for escaping his unjust incarceration.

👉 解析

❶ 這句話由以下兩句構成：

(1) The seagulls gave Daedalus an idea for escaping his unjust incarceration.

(2) Daedalus and Icarus spent their days watchingthe seagulls float freely through the air

值得注意的是：先行詞 seagulls 是第二個句子的附屬子句裡面的受詞，因此合併後看到 watching 後面馬上接 float，會產生動詞重覆出現的錯覺。換句話說，關係代名詞的先行詞不見得是主要子句的名詞，附屬子句的也可以。例如：I am taking the medicine which I think works very well!（我正在服用的藥，我覺得蠻有效的。）

# Icarus and Daedalus (2)

# 伊卡魯斯和泰達路斯（2）

閱讀原文：試用 3 分鐘的時間念完文章，記得先把中文遮上，並翻頁看題目問什麼。計時開始！

### Icarus and Daedalus (2)

When he floated back to earth, Daedalus immediately began to **mold** a set of wings for his son. Soon father and son were prepared to take flight, but before taking off, Daedalus warned Icarus neither to fly too high, because the heat of the sun would melt the wax, nor too low, because the sea **foam** would wet the feathers. As was the case with wayward children, Icarus turned a deaf ear to whatever his elders said. The joy he felt over his escape and the power of his youth **prompted** him to sail higher and higher into the air. Nothing could **quench** his desire to reach the heavens.

The higher Icarus flew, the warmer the air became.

Gradually the wings grew **limp**, and then they began to **disintegrate**. Feathers **fluttered** to the ground. Icarus tried flapping his wings harder and harder, but it was of no use. Icarus fell headlong into the sea. Hearing his son's cries, Daedalus began searching for him, but all he found were hundreds of feathers floating on the sea.

## 伊卡魯斯和泰達路斯（2）

　　當泰達路斯飛回地面時，立即著手為兒子造出一對翅膀。很快父子倆就準備要溜之大吉了，可是要起飛前，泰達路斯警告伊卡魯斯不要飛得太高，因為太陽的熱度會把蠟融化掉，但是也不要飛得太低，因為海水泡沫會把羽毛打濕。伊卡魯斯就跟任性孩子一樣，對長輩所說的話都馬耳東風。逃出生天的喜悅與年輕的活力促使他飛得愈來愈高，什麼也壓抑不住他想飛到天堂的渴望。

　　伊卡魯斯飛得愈高，空氣就愈溫暖。翅膀逐漸鬆軟了，然後開始解體，羽毛飄落地面。伊卡魯斯翅膀愈拍愈大力，但是卻徒勞無功，頭下腳上栽進海裡。泰達路斯聽到兒子叫聲，開始找他，但是只發現成百上千根羽毛漂浮在海面上。

從拆解文化題目，看關係子句的角色

**All of the following are mentioned in the passage EXCEPT**

(A) As Icarus soared up into the sky, he became hard of hearing.

(B) Icarus flew too close to the sun, the heat of which made his wings dissolve.

(C) At the sound of Icarus crying for help, Daedalus flew to his rescue, but to no avail.

(D) Icarus ended up dead.

以下哪一點本文並未提及

(A) 伊卡魯斯飛上天時，變成重聽了。

(B) 伊卡魯斯飛得離太陽太近，熱度使得羽毛分解掉。

(C) 一聽到伊卡魯斯的求救聲，泰達路斯飛來救他，但是無功而返。

(D) 伊卡魯斯最後死掉了。

解析

答案│(A)

❶ 這一題答案在 As was the case with wayward children, Icarus turned a deaf ear to whatever his elders said.這

句話。其中 turn a deaf ear to「對……充耳不聞」這個片語；相對也有 turn a blind eye to「對……視而不見」。

❷ wayward = way + ward。-ward 是表示方向的字尾，意即 turn，如常見的 toward、forward、backward；字根 way 即 away；照字根結構解讀就是 turn away。「任性的、倔強的」人是不會乖乖接受規勸的，不是轉身離去就是別過臉去。

❸ (A) 選項 hard of hearing 即「重聽、聽力不靈」，跟題目的 turn a deaf ear to 八竿子打不著，答案要不是 (A)，還會是哪個？

❹ (B) 選項可以改成 Icarus flew too close to the sun, whose heat made his wings dissolve.。

❺ (C) 選項 avail = a(to) + vail(value)，字根 vail 即 value「價值」。發揮出應有價值時，才會讓人覺得有「助益、效用」，有一種值回票價的意味；to no avail 得不到應有的代價，所以是「徒勞無功」。形容詞 available「有效的、可得到的」比較常見。

❻ (D) 選項 end up 跟 turn out、come out、wind up、prove 一樣，後面接的都是最終的結果。

❶ As was the case with wayward children, Icarus turned a deaf ear towhatever his elders said.

👉 **解析**

❶ as 當準關係代名詞時，其先行詞可以是它前面的主要子句，也可以是它後面的主要子句，本句便是後者這種情況。這種用法跟 which 很像，但是差異就在 as 可以置於句首，但 which 不行。換句話說，本句也可以寫成：

Icarus turned a deaf ear to whatever his elders said, as was the case with wayward children.

= Icarus turned a deaf ear to whatever his elders said, which was the case with wayward children.

再舉一例：

She is kind, as is known to us.

= She is kind, which is known to us.

= As is known to us, she is kind.（眾所皆知，她人很好。）

❷ 本句的 whatever 是複合關係代名詞，複合關係代名詞 = 先行詞 + 關係代名詞，這個 whatever 的先行詞就是 anything，關係代名詞是 that 或 which。本句的 whatever his elders said 是 turned a deaf ear to 的受詞。注意：複合

關係代名詞是用主格、受格，還是所有格取決於從屬子句，而非主要子句，跟關係代名詞一樣。例如：

Give it to anyone who wants it.= Give it to **whoever** wants it.（把它送給任何要它的人。）

I will welcome anyone whom you invite.= I will welcome **whomever** you invite.（我會歡迎你所邀請的任何人。）

❷ (Soon father and son were prepared to take flight), but {before taking off, Daedalus warned Icarus [neither to fly too high, (because the heat of the sun would melt the wax)],[nor too low, (because the sea foam would wet the feathers)]}.

### 📖 解析

❶ but 連接兩句，後面那句又是 neither…nor…，又是 because，把整個句子拉得很長，但是句意應該不難理解。neither..nor…是對等連接詞，nor 後面原來有 to fly，因為跟 neither 後面的 to fly 一樣，所以省略掉了。

❷ 在名詞成雙成對出現的成語裡，常常會省略冠詞，所以 father and son 都不需要加任何冠詞，此外還有：day and night（夜以繼日）、year after year（一年又一年）、step by step（逐步）、from door to door（挨家挨戶）、from head to foot（從頭到腳）……等。

# Across and Down (1)

## 縱橫無阻（1）

 閱讀原文：試用 3 分鐘的時間念完文章，記得先把中文遮上，並翻頁看題目問什麼。計時開始！

**Across and Down (1)**

The first crossword puzzle was a **whimsical** holiday gift of sorts. Arthur Wynne, a newspaper editor, was looking for a way to **enliven** the 1913 Christmas edition of the New York World Sunday magazine. He drew a diamond-shaped grid and fashioned a puzzle of thirty-two interlocking words that he called "Word Cross." Although it became a regular Sunday feature, the game did not really take off until 1924, when Simon and Schuster published the first book devoted to the puzzles.

It wasn't long before solving crossword puzzles became a national **compulsion**. There were few people but got carried away by the most popular and widespread word game in the world. Sales of dictionaries and **thesauri** rose, and restaurants printed the black-and-white grids on the backs of their menus. These early puzzles were relatively simple, consisting mainly of one-word solutions based on current events and general information. Over the years, crosswords became unimaginative and predictable.

## 縱橫無阻（ 1 ）

　　第一個填字遊戲只是一個異想天開、不入流的假日附加版面。報社編輯亞瑟魏恩想找個玩意，讓 1913 年紐約世界週日雜誌的聖誕節版更生動一點。他畫出菱形方格，讓 32 個單字互相交疊，設計成一個謎題，稱之為「縱橫字謎」，雖然就此定期成為假日版的一項特色，但是要到 1924 年賽門和休斯特出版了第一本字謎專書，這種遊戲才風靡起來。

　　不久玩填字遊戲在全國掀起一股熱潮，幾乎每個人都迷上這個全世界人氣最強、流傳最廣的文字遊戲。字典銷售量扶搖直上，餐廳甚至在菜單背面都印上黑白空格。早期填字遊戲都相當簡單，答案主要都一個字，以時事、常識為主。幾年下來，填字遊戲變得想像力貧乏而且很容易猜。

從拆解文化題目，看關係子句的角色

**Which of the following best expresses the essential information in the underlined sentence? Incorrect answer choices change the meaning in important ways or leave out essential information.**

(A) Though popular and widespread in other countries, the word game appealed to a very small group of people in America.

(B) Despite its popularity worldwide, the crossword puzzle was illegal in America.

(C) The crossword puzzle won massive popularity.

(D) Most crossword puzzles were so hard that very few people could work them out.

以下哪一句最能表達出劃底線句子的基本訊息？不正確的答案選項會以重要方式改變句義，或者遺漏基本訊息

(A) 雖然這個文字遊戲在其他國家大受歡迎而且十分普及，但是在美國只吸引一小撮人。

(B) 雖然填字遊戲全球炙手可熱，但是在美國卻是違法的。

(C) 填字遊戲人氣炒得強強滾。

(D) 大部分填字遊戲非常難，極少人解得出來。

### ☞ 解析

答案 | (C)

❶ get carried away 照字面解釋是「被帶走了」，那麼被帶走的是什麼？就是心思。太過專注於某一件事而做過了頭，或忘乎所以，或是當情緒戰勝了理智時，都算是 get carried away。例如：The teacher warned his students not to get carried away by the emotion of the occasion.（老師警告學生不要受一時情緒所左右。）

這句話將 get carried away 套進準關係代名詞 but 的句子裡，整句話大意就是一 很少人沒被填字遊戲這股熱潮沖昏頭，那當然是指 crossword puzzle 人氣當紅不讓，所以答案是 (C)。

❷ 你或許不知道 massive 是什麼意思，但是一定知道數學 max 代表極大值。而且凡是用過 Microsoft Office，尤其是 Excel，一定都知道 macro「巨集」。英文很多 ma- 開頭的單字意思都「大」有關，例如：**mass**「大量的」、**magnate**「巨頭」、**majestic**「宏偉的」、**magnify**「放大」。

❸ 從緊接其後的句子說字典跟著水漲船高熱賣起來，就可以判斷不管像 (A) 所述曲高和寡，還是 (B) 所述非法，甚至是 (D) 所述難度很高，都不可能導致這種結果。

ch 1

ch 2

ch 3

從拆解文化題目，看關係子句的角色

ch 4

ch 5

ch 6

❶ There were few people but got carried away by the most popular and widespread word game in the world.

👉 解析

❶ 這句話最重要的關鍵就在準關係代名詞 but，意思是「除了…之外」。準關係代名詞才三個而已：but、as、than；but 常常跟否定字眼連用，例如 no、little、hardly；than 當然跟形影不離的絕配比較級連用；as 則是和 the same、such、as 老搭檔連用。but 本身就有排除的意味，再跟否定字眼聯袂現身時，難免會出現雙重否定負負得正的現象，這一點千萬要注意。例如：

There is no person but loves money.

= There is no person that does not love money.

（沒有不愛錢的人）

❷ 關係代名詞在子句裡面不是做主詞就是做受詞，準關係代名詞也不例外。然而因為準關係代名詞曝光率遠不及一般關係代名詞，讀者會感到比較陌生，因此碰到這種句子時，會產生彷彿缺少主詞或受詞的錯覺。例如：Don't give children more money than is needed.（不要給孩子多於他們所有需

要的錢。）

❷ Although it became a regular Sunday feature, the game did not really take off until 1924, [when Simon and Schuster published the first book (devoted to the puzzles)].

👉 解析

❶ 後面中括號框起來的關係副詞 when 帶領子句做 1924 的補語，這個 when 意思是「那時」，說明那一年這兩個作家合力出版了第一本填字遊戲的書籍。

❷ 小括號框起來的 devoted to the puzzles 前面省略掉 which was。

❸ devote 的字根 vote 是它們的表親：很多場合免不了都要發聲說話，**vow**「誓約、發誓」也是在說話，但是是在神前承諾，這就類似我們的剁雞頭。在神明面前剁雞頭發誓，還敢黑白講嗎？因此 **vouch** 就是「保證」。**vote**「投票」。民主時代投票沒什麼了不起，但是古時候只有極少數人擁有選舉權時，投票前必須先對上天發誓，絕不因威脅利誘而玷污自己神聖的一票。**votary**「信徒、修道人」神前許諾放下所有貪戀、捨棄執著，將自己全部 **devote**「奉獻」給上帝，這才是 **devout**「虔誠的」、**votive**「奉獻的」。

# Unit 3-8

# Across and Down (2)

## 縱橫無阻（2）

閱讀原文：試用 3 分鐘的時間念完文章，記得先把中文遮上，並翻頁看題目問什麼。計時開始！

### Across and Down (2)

It is ironic that the crossword puzzle **revival** was led by a major newspaper that had held out against the craze. In 1924 the New York Times had **bemoaned** the game's **prevalence** as "a primitive form of mental exercise" and predicted its swift demise. Obviously unsuccessful in **extirpating** crosswords, the Times finally **capitulated** and published its own puzzle in 1942. Its Sunday and daily versions, introduced a few years later, soon established themselves as the standard of excellence.

The New York Times puzzle editors were **instrumental** in establishing such golden rules as continue to govern the creation of crosswords: the grid must be entirely interconnected; the briefer the clue, the better; and no two-letter words are permitted. It is also considered bad form to have two **obscure** words **intersect**. Puzzle makers are expected to avoid "crosswordese"–**abstruse** words that, because of convenient vowel-consonant combinations, have been overused. Despite these rules, some crosswords are difficult enough to tempt the frustrated to abandon their personal ethics temporarily, and turn to the solution page for some answers.

## 縱橫無阻（2）

很諷刺的是，填字遊戲的風雲再起竟然由一家反對這股熱潮的大報發難。1924 年紐約時報對這遊戲的盛行深表遺憾，認為它只是「心智體操的原始模式」，並預測很快會銷聲匿跡。紐約時報這樣唱衰填字遊戲，很明顯並沒有，最後只好認輸，而且還在 1942 年發行了自己的填字遊戲。幾年以後推出的周日版和每日版更是樹立出優秀的典範。

紐約時報的字謎編輯在建立字謎遊戲的金科玉律上起了推波助瀾的作用，至今設計填字遊戲時，還是照著這些規則走：黑白框格必須全部互相連結；提示愈簡短愈好；不准使用才兩個字母的單字。兩個隱晦難解的字眼互相交錯也被認為差勁的格式。設計字謎的人也應該避免「陳腔濫調」，亦即為了母音子音的組合方便，而過度使用的艱澀單字。儘管有這些規則，有些填字遊戲

從拆解文化題目，看關係子句的角色

還是難到足以讓那些灰頭土臉的玩家暫時撇下個人道德，直接翻到解答頁看答案。

 **考題演練及解析**

**According to this passage, what make a good crossword puzzle, EXCEPT that**

(A) avoid the group of words frequently found in crossword puzzles but seldom found in daily conversation.

(B) two difficult words should never be allowed to cross.

(C) all the words in the grid should connect with each other.

(D) all words should be at least two letters long.

根據本文，好的填字遊戲不包含哪個條件

(A) 填字遊戲中經常見到，但是日常會話卻極少使用的字眼要儘量避免。

(B) 不要讓兩個深奧的字眼交錯。

(C) 黑白框格所有單字應該要互相交會連結。

(D) 所有單字應該至少要有兩個字母。

### 解析

答案｜(D)

❶ 這一題答案幾乎涵蓋最後一段全部，開頭第一句提到三條規則，緊接其後的兩句又各自提到一條，整理如下：

(1) the grid must be entirely interconnected

(2) the briefer the clue, the better

(3) no two-letter words are permitted

(4) don't have two obscure words intersect

(5) avoid "crosswordese"

回頭看四個選項，可以發現：

(A) 對應到 (5)。根據 crosswordese 後面的同位語可以得知，這些辭彙 abstruse「深奧難懂的」，證明生活中極少用到，可是在填字遊戲中卻 overuse 了。

(B) 對應到 (4)。(C) 對應到 (1)。

(D) 似乎對應到 (3)，其實不然。填字遊戲的答案當然不可能只有一個字母，原來規則又說不要使用兩個字母的單字，因此所有單字起碼要有三個字母，才算符合條件。(D) 所述錯誤，答案就是它了。

❷ 填字遊戲無非就是一堆縱橫交錯的黑白方格，看起來不是跟烤肉架很像嗎？這就是何以本文會出現 grid「烤架、鐵絲網、格子」的原因。被格柵、鐵絲網卡住自然就動彈不得，所以 gridlock 就是「僵局、交通阻塞」。同源字彙還有 grill「烤架、烤肉」。

## 深度應用分析：對付閱讀就是要化「繁」為「簡」。先刪去( )、[ ] 內的文字，找出主要的主詞和動詞！

**❶** The New York Times puzzle editors were instrumental in establishing such golden rules[as continue to govern the creation of crosswords: (the grid must be entirely interconnected); (the briefer the clue, the better); and (no two-letter words are permitted)].

## 解析

**❶** 這句話又出現準關係代名詞，只是這一次改成 as，把整個句子拉得很長，主要是介紹紐約時報所樹立的三條填字遊戲的設計規則。

**❷** 有些場合 such 和 so 可以互換，例如 such a wonderful miracle = so wonderful a miracle

可是碰到複數名詞或不可數名詞時，一定用 such。像本句的 such golden rules 就不能改用 so。例如：such nice weather 或 such wonderful miracles。唯一例外是後面緊接 many、much，這時反而一定用 so。例如：

Could you imagine learning so many languages?

（你能想像要學這麼多種語言嗎？）

Cicadas make so much noise.

（蟬發出很多噪音。）

可是假如 many 不是緊接在後，而是置於前面，那麼用 such 倒是不妨。例如：

This isn't the only story of battered women. Many such cases are reported every day.

（這並非受虐婦女的唯一案例，每天都有很多類似的。）

❷ Despite these rules, some crosswords are difficult enough [to tempt the frustrated (to abandon their personal ethics temporarily), and (turn to the solution page for some answers)].

### 👉 解析

❶ 形容詞前面出現 the 是泛指所有那種情況的人，假如是主詞，必須視為複數，譬如 the sick 病人、the poor 窮人、the old 老人、the unemployed 失業的人，因此 the frustrated 就是指那些玩填字遊戲玩到像洩氣皮球一樣的玩家。

❷ the frustrated 後面接兩個不定詞片語，意即玩到垂頭喪氣的玩家忍不住去做兩件事：個人道德先擺一旁；偷看答案。

# Graffiti: Making the Leap from Illegal to Legal (1)

## 街頭塗鴉：從非法到合法（1）

 閱讀原文：試用 3 分鐘的時間念完文章，記得先把中文遮上，並翻頁看題目問什麼。計時開始！

**Graffiti: Making the Leap from Illegal to Legal (1)**

Speaking of spray-paint scribbles, slogans, or obscenities spoiling the urban landscape, graffiti writers have become the scourge of politicians and the police. Under the **aegis** of neighborhood planning boards and even some mayors, however, what was once **vandalism** is now being converted into community art.

Many wall-writers, tired of **wielding** spray-paint cans and **dodging** the police, have, on their own, branched into safer and more remunerative forms of art. Some have redirected their efforts from buildings, bridges, and fences to T-shirts, theatrical stage sets, and compact disc covers. Others have adapted their messages to advertising, gracing the walls of commercial establishments with graffiti-style signs.

It is the **amnesty** programs for graffiti writers that have been most successful in turning eyesores into art. In many large cities, former scrawlers now work to beautify the walls they once **ravaged**. Part government agency, part social service organization, and part art workshop, each group paints its town in rich **hues** while learning discipline, responsibility, and cooperation.

## 街頭塗鴉：從非法到合法（1）

一提到破壞都市景觀的噴漆塗鴉、口號、猥褻文字，塗鴉藝術家早已是政客和警方的心腹大患。然而就在社區規劃委員會，甚至某些市長的保護傘下，過去視為蓄意破壞的行為現在正轉變為社區藝術。

許多塗鴉藝術家對肆意揮灑噴漆罐、跟警方玩躲貓貓深感厭倦，早已自己衍化出一些安全感更高、報酬率更好的藝術形式。有些將精力從建築、橋樑、圍牆轉移到 T 恤、戲院舞台佈置、光碟封面；也有一些將想表達的訊息轉化為廣告，以塗鴉風格的標誌來美化廣告牆。

這個對塗鴉藝術家的特赦專案非常成功的將眾人的眼中釘轉為藝術。在許多大都市，洗心革面的塗鴉客目前在以往作怪的牆上認真妝點美化。部分是政府代理機構、部分是服務組織、部分是藝術工作室，每個團體都以豐富的色彩來塗抹自己的鄉鎮，同

時也學習到自律、負責、合作。

 **考題演練及解析**

**Which of the following best expresses the essential information in the underlined sentence? Incorrect answer choices change the meaning in important ways or leave out essential information.**

(A) When talking about what they have done to disfigure the city, graffiti writers have long been the target that local authorities try to crack down on.

(B) Street artists remain a nuisance issue for cities when it comes to wall paintings

(C) If people refer to graffiti messages, law-enforcement officials around the city will prosecute muralists with harsh sentences.

(D) Because graffiti vandals mention their doodles, police officers have imposed sanctions on them.

以下哪一句最能表達出劃底線句子的基本訊息？不正確的答案選項會以重要方式改變句義，或者遺漏基本訊息

(A) 塗鴉藝術家一談到自己醜化城市的所作所為時，老早就是地方當局所要取締的目標。

(B) 一提到牆壁塗鴉，塗鴉畫家一直都是所有城市的頭痛人物。

(C) 假如人們一提到塗鴉的訊息，城市的執法官員就會以重刑起訴塗鴉藝術家。

(D) 因為塗鴉藝術家提到自己的傑作，警察便處罰他們。

👉 **解析**

答案｜**(B)**

❶ 要是把 speaking of 當作是一般分詞構句，誤以為 graffiti writers 是它的主詞，就會掉入此題陷阱。開頭的 Speaking of…其實是分詞的慣用語，又叫做「無人稱獨立分詞片語」，文法上應該視為介系詞，意思是「説到……」。由於是慣用語，就代表它本來就固定這麼説，不必考慮主詞是什麼，也無須理會主被動關係，跟一般分詞構句大大不同。

❷ TOEFL 的句構重述題既然焦點全放在一句，其他部分都不考，因此作答時非得字斟句酌不可。仔細看這題四個選項，會發現對 graffiti writers have become the scourge of politicians and the police 的詮釋大同小異，彼此間的差異全部都在對 Speaking of spray-paint scribbles, slogans, or obscenities spoiling the urban landscape 這部分的解讀。換句話說，這一題主要就是考 speaking of 的用法與意思。

❸ (B) 選項 when it comes to 意即「一談到……」，跟 speaking of 可以畫上等號，因此答案就是(B)。注意：這個 it 並不代替哪一個名詞，而是這個句型天生就是這樣子。

## 深度應用分析：對付閱讀就是要化「繁」為「簡」。先刪去( )、[ ] 內的文字，找出主要的主詞和動詞！

❶ [Speaking of spray-paint scribbles, slogans, or obscenities (spoiling the urban landscape)], graffiti writers have become the scourge of politicians and the police.

### 解析

❶ 分詞片語 spoiling the urban landscape 是要修飾前面提到的 spray-paint scribbles、slogans、obscenities

❷ 除了 speaking of 以外，其他作介系詞用的分詞慣用語還有：talking about 說到；judging from/by 由……看來；depending on 根據；according to 根據；based on 基於；compared with 與……比較；owing to 因為。例如：

Judging from the cheers, the Yankees must have won the game.

（從歡呼聲來判斷，洋基隊一定贏了比賽。）

Based on these reasons, I chose to study abroad in England.

（基於這些因素，我選擇去英國留學。）

❸ 上述分詞慣用語跟一般分詞構句不一樣，並沒有省略掉主詞、連接詞，也沒必要考慮到主動、被動的關係

❷ Many wall-writers, (tired of wielding spray-paint cans and dodging the police), have, on their own, branched into safer and more remunerative forms of art.

## ☞ 解析

❶ 表被動的 tired of…分詞片語是要修飾前面的 Many wall-writers，也可以把這分詞片語放在句首。

❷ 這句話原來應該是這樣──Because many wall-writers were tired of wielding spray-paint cans and dodging the police, they have, on their own, branched into safer and more remunerative forms of art.

→ 改寫流程如下：因為目標是把兩句濃縮成一句，連接詞再也派不上用場，所以第一步就是大刀一揮把 because 砍了。因為兩個句子主詞 many wall-writers 是同一對象，所以刪掉附屬子句的主詞，把主要子句的主詞 they 替換成 many wall-writers。下來由於單靠 tired 就能呈現被動涵義，因此 be 動詞 were 也沒保留的必要。最後，一個全新的分詞構句終於變身成功了！

💡 閱讀原文：試用 **3** 分鐘的時間念完文章，記得先把中文遮上，並翻頁看題目問什麼。計時開始！

街頭塗鴉：從非法到合法（**2**）

(A) Beginning by obtaining the necessary permission to use unsightly fences, abandoned buildings, and blank walls as the **canvases** for astonishing **murals**, the street artists seek ideas from local residents so that the paintings will reflect neighborhood heritage and values. (B) Hours of effort are required to turn a vision into reality.(C) Professional artists may be hired to transfer the design to the larger surface, but it is the ex-wall writers and members of the community who add the color and the detail to **exotic** tropical gardens, portraits of illustrious sports stars, and memorial scenes from history. (D)

Each of the murals is a treasured **asset** and a source

of pride for its neighborhood. Like giant postcards or living museum walls, these murals carry a message that everyone can understand. By channeling the talents of graffiti artists into community art color triumphs over **drabness** in constructive self-expression. Seen from a different perspective, graffiti, if managed well, is an excellent way to add color and **vibrancy** to public spaces.

## 街頭塗鴉：從非法到合法（2）

(A) 因為要把不雅觀的圍牆、廢棄建築、空白牆壁當作是超大畫作的畫布，所以就從取得它們的使用權開始，這些塗鴉藝術家從當地居民身上尋求點子，以便這些畫作可以反映出整個街坊的傳承與價值。(B) 還需要幾個小時的努力才能將想像化為現實。(C) 雖然或許要請專業畫家把圖樣描到壁面，但是最後還是要靠塗鴉藝術家和社區成員來上色，為異國風味的熱帶花園、大名鼎鼎的運動明星肖像、歷史紀念場景畫上細節。(D)

每幅壁畫既是珍藏的資產而且也是街坊鄰居深感驕傲的對象。這些壁畫宛如巨大的明信片或活生生的博物館外牆，帶著一個大家都懂得訊息。將塗鴉藝術家的才華導向社區藝術，在建設性的自我表達中，色彩戰勝了單調。從不同角度來看，妥善管理的話，街頭塗鴉是一種為公共場所添加色彩與活力的絕妙方法。

1

2

3

4

從拆解藝術、人文類題目，看分詞構句、介系詞的角色

5

6

 **考題演練及解析**

Look at the four letters that indicate where the following sentence could be added to the passage.

**The design conception refined, graffiti writers and neighborhood volunteers erect a scaffold, scrape and whitewash the surface, and create a grid for the sketch.**

Where could the sentence best fit?

看看文章裡四個字母，哪個地方可以把下面句子安插進去

整個設計概念萃取出來以後，塗鴉藝術家和鄰里義工搭蓋鷹架，把表面刮除清洗乾淨，畫出素描用的方格。

這句子放哪裡最合適？

**解析**

答案｜(C)

❶ 題目這一段主要是陳述合法街頭塗鴉的創作過程。插入句題型碰到這種平鋪直述的文章等於是送分題，因為只要掌握好時間先後順序，肯定手到擒來。

❷ 從題目句子來分析，**the design conception** 三個字暗示整個塗鴉圖案構思出來了，軟體工程告一段落；後面主要子句說明之後塗鴉藝術家和義工攜手進行硬體工程。綜合以上線

索，本句應該處於整個創作過程的中間，無形的即將轉換成有形的，不是初期，也不是末期。

❸ (A)選項一看就知道不可能，因為隨後第一句劈頭就是 Beginning 叫我第一名，何況後面所提的內容都是取得許可、和居民商議協調等先行作業，一看就知道一定不是主題句。

❹ 從 (D) 選項前一句可以知道整個塗鴉已經完工了，因此絕不可能是 (D)。

❺ 那麼是 (B) 還是 (C)？Hours of effort are required to turn a vision into reality 這句的 reality 暗示之前還是處於無形的階段，可是題目句的 scaffold、surface、grid 字眼意味已經進入有形階段，所以要放進 (C) 才對。

## ⚙️ 深度應用分析：對付閱讀就是要化「繁」為「簡」。先刪去( )、[ ] 內的文字，找出主要的主詞和動詞！

**❶** The design conception refined, graffiti writers and neighborhood volunteers erect a scaffold, scrape and whitewash the surface, and create a grid for the sketch.

### 👈 解析

**❶** 本句是附屬連接詞引導的副詞子句簡化成的獨立分詞構句。這句話本來是這樣：Once (the design conception is refined), (graffiti writers and neighborhood volunteers erect a scaffold, scrape and whitewash the surface, and create a grid for the sketch).連接詞 Once 連接兩句。後面那句話敘述了塗鴉藝術家和鄰里義工所做的三件事：erect a scaffold 搭鷹架；scrape and whitewash the surface 刮除清洗外牆；create a grid for the sketch 劃出素描方格

**❷** 把連接詞 Once 省略掉。因為兩句話主詞 the design conception、graffiti writers and neighborhood volunteers 不一樣，所以都要保留。原來的 is 改成 being，因為單憑過去分詞 refined 就有被動的涵義，所以沒有意思的 being 也一併去掉。這就是獨立分詞構句。

❷ [Beginning by obtaining the necessary permission to use (unsightly fences), (abandoned buildings), and (blank walls) as the canvases for astonishing murals], the street artists seek ideas from local residents (so that the paintings will reflect neighborhood heritage and values).

### 👉 解析

❶ 中括號裡面的三個小括號是說明塗鴉藝術家創作前必須先取得的三種許可：unsightly fences、abandoned buildings、blank walls。最後面小括號 so that 表目的，指出塗鴉藝術在規範下，汲取居民想法，力求把街坊的傳承與價值表現出來，造成塗鴉藝術家、當地居民、市政管理機構三贏的結果。

❷ 這句話本來是這樣：The street artists begin by obtaining the necessary permission to use unsightly fences, abandoned buildings, and blank walls as the canvases for astonishing murals. They seek ideas from local residents so that the paintings will reflect neighborhood heritage and values.

因為兩句主詞都是 the street artists，所以先省略第一句話的主詞；由於原來動詞 begin 是主動，因此改成現在分詞 beginning；兩句合體完成。

# Baseball Card Collection (1)

## 棒球卡收藏樂（1）

 閱讀原文：試用 3 分鐘的時間念完文章，記得先把中文遮上，並翻頁看題目問什麼。計時開始！

### Baseball Card Collection (1)

Issued in the 1880s, the first mass-produced baseball cards were sold with everything from gum to dog food. The publishers' **inchoate** notions of what the cards should contain seem rather **peculiar** today. These early cards bore little resemblance to current laser-printed collectibles. Lacking biography or statistics on the back, they sported only a studio photograph of a player swinging at a ball suspended on a string.

These earliest cards are not as valuable as most people think. With only a few exceptions, yesterday's players fall short of both the flashiness and the records of more current stars. Furthermore, although the early cards meet the demands of age and rarity, they usually lack an important variable in determining worth condition. **Pristine** cards are straight-out-of-the-package perfect: sharp corners, **crisp** edges, and brilliant colors. Even the tiniest **defect** indelibly labels a card as damaged goods. A card handled but not abused commands only 20 to 30 percent of the price of one in mint condition. Shoeboxes have given way to specially designed holders that offer protection from the elements.

## 棒球卡收藏樂（**1**）

第一批大量生產的棒球卡是 1880 年代發行的，當初只要買任何東西，從口香糖到狗食，通通附送一張。早期發行商對棒球卡上面應該要涵蓋什麼內容的想法，在今天看來似乎相當奇特。這些早期的棒球卡跟當前雷射印刷的珍藏卡片幾乎完全不同。背面沒有球員生平介紹和統計數據，上面只印著一位球員對著綁在細繩上的球揮棒的相館照片。

最早期的棒球卡其實不像大多數人想像那麼值錢。目前棒球明星的花俏與表現紀錄，過去的球員都付之闕如。此外，雖然早期棒球卡符合年代久遠與稀有性的需求條件，但是判斷價值時，通常都沒有很重要的浮動標準。原封不動的卡片可說是有如剛拆封般的完美無瑕：邊角完整、側邊硬挺、色彩鮮艷。即使有一絲絲缺憾，一張卡片也難免被標示為瑕疵商品。一張卡片即使僅碰觸過，但是並沒有缺損，價值只有全新狀態卡片的百分之二、三十。鞋盒從此代之以特殊設計的珍藏本，以保護卡片免於因自然因素而走樣。

 考題演練及解析

**According to this passage, which of the following was NOT true of the early baseball cards?**

(A) In the early times baseball cards were offered as a giveaway.

(B) Baseball cards in top condition sell for more money than those with some flaws.

(C) Figuring out a vintage baseball card's value is not a simple task.

(D) The early baseball cards featured only players posing in a ballpark.

根據這篇文章，以下有關早期棒球卡的陳述是不對的

(A) 早期棒球卡是當作贈品給的。

(B) 頂級棒球卡比有瑕疵的棒球卡賣更多錢。

(C) 要計算老式棒球卡的價值並非輕而易舉。

(D) 早期棒球卡上面只印著在球場裡擺姿勢的球員。

解析

答案｜(D)

❶ (A) 關鍵就在第一段第一句…the first mass-produced baseball cards were sold with everything from gum to dog food，既然棒球卡是 were sold with everything from gum to dog food，就意味那時只是隨物附贈的玩意。

❷ 從第二段的 A card handled but not abused commands only 20 to 30 percent of the price of one in mint condition 這句話可以知道 (A) 陳述也對。注意這個 mint 可不是薄荷，也不是什麼造幣廠，而是「全新的」。

❸ (C) 關鍵就在第二段…they usually lack an important variable in determining worth condition。既然早期棒球卡 lack an important variable，要 determining worth condition 當然很困難。注意這裡用 vintage「葡萄產量」當形容詞來修飾棒球卡，意味如同葡萄酒愈陳愈香一樣，早期棒球卡也愈收藏愈值錢。

❹ (D) 選項說棒球卡上印著球員在 ballpark「球場」擺 pose，對應第一段最後一句…they sported only a studio photograph of a player swinging at a ball suspended on a string。其中 a studio photograph 便是關鍵，studio 是畫家、雕刻家、攝影家的工作室，本文應該是指照相館。換句話說，那些球員照片是在照相館拍的，而不是球場。(D) 所述不符，為本題答案！

*ei* 1
*ei* 2
*ei* 3
*ei* 4
從拆解藝術、人文類題目，看分詞構句、介系詞的角色
*ei* 5
*ei* 6

❶ Lacking biography or statistics on the back, they sported only a studio photograph of a player [swinging at a ball(suspended on a string)].

👉 **解析**

❶ 這句話又是分詞構句，句首的 Lacking 是現在分詞。

❷ 小括號框起來的 suspended on a string 修飾前面的 ball；中括號框起來的 swinging at a ball…修飾前面的 player。

❸ 其實 sport 就是 **disport**「娛樂、嬉戲」；從字形來看，只是原本字首 dis-簡化成 s 而已；從字義來看，運動也算一種娛樂，而且有些辭彙都可以見證 sport 和 disport 的關係，例如：spoilsport「掃興鬼」會 spoil the fun；make sport of「嘲笑」等於 make fun of；sporting house 並非健身房，而是「妓院」，因為那是尋歡作樂的地方。可是 disport 為什麼是娛樂呢？字首 dis-意即 away，字根 port 意即 carry。在 port 有船 carry 旅客；在 airport 有飛機 carry 旅客。同理，**portable**「可攜帶的」，而 **portly** 則是指一個人 carry 太多游泳圈、贅肉，所以是「肥胖的」。

言歸正傳，照字根來看 disport 可以解讀成（把注意力）carry away，娛樂就是把注意力從正經事 carry away 的玩意。這句話 sport 意思是刊載 carry away 大眾眼球的球員照片。

❷ A card (handled but not abused) commands only 20 to 30 percent of the price of one in mint condition.

👉 解析

❶ 修飾 A card 的分詞片語 handled but not abused 前面省略了 which is；後面的 one 是代替前面的 A card。

❷ 這句話有幾個很普通的單字，但是套用在這句的意思跟尋常不太一樣：

(1) handle 一般是「處理、控制」，但是這裡要翻成「碰觸」。例如：Wash your hands before you handle food.（洗完手再拿食物。）

(2) command 一般是「命令、控制」，但是這裡要翻成「值得」。例如：His bravery commands our respect.（他的勇敢值得我們尊敬。）

(3) in mint condition 原先是指錢幣剛從造幣廠出來時嶄新的狀況，後來擴大到各種東西。例如：
This toy is nearly flawless and is considered to be in mint condition.（這本漫畫幾乎完美無瑕，可以視為全新。）

ch 1
ch 2
ch 3
ch 4
ch 5
ch 6
從拆解藝術、人文類題目，看分詞構句、介系詞的角色

# Baseball Card Collection (2)

## 棒球卡收藏樂（2）

閱讀原文：試用 **3** 分鐘的時間念完文章，記得先
把中文遮上，並翻頁看題目問什麼。計時開始！

### Baseball Card Collection (2)

(A) As **vying** for choice merchandise, collectors and dealers **speculate** on players' futures.(B) **Rookie** cards of players who were later elected to the Hall of Fame are thus among the most valuable. The cards of power hitters do better than those of other players. Pitchers are the biggest risk of all, because they are always in danger of career-threatening arm injuries. (C) Once the pastime of grade school kids and originally a simple hobby with few rules, collecting baseball cards has become big business, and gleeful hobbyists have been transfigured into serious-minded investors. (D)

Putting money into baseball cards is **akin** to

speculating on the stock market. There is no guarantee that the investment will maintain even a **faint** reflection of the cost. Baseball-card enthusiasts agree, however, that it is better to be stuck with a collection of their favorite heroes than with a bunch of equally worthless stock **certificates**.

## 棒球卡收藏樂（2）

(A) 收藏家和賣家為選擇貨品競價時，要仔細評估球員們的未來發展。(B) 有些菜鳥球員以後可能入選棒球名人堂，他們的新人卡也因此最有價值。強打者的棒球卡比其他球員賣相更好。所有球員之中風險最高的莫過於投手，因為他們一直處於手臂傷害的危險之中，而這種傷害會威脅到其職業生涯。(C) 收集棒球卡過去曾經是國小學童的消遣，原來只是沒什麼遊戲規則的簡單嗜好，如今卻變成大買賣，原本怡情養性的業餘愛好人士也轉型成精打細算的投資人。(D)

砸錢去買棒球卡跟炒股票差不多，無法保證投資可以反映出些微回本。然而棒球卡的玩家都同意，與其擁有一疊同樣都一文不值的股票證書，倒不如擁有一整套自己最喜歡的球星棒球卡。

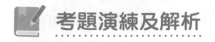 **考題演練及解析**

Look at the four letters that indicate where the following sentence could be added to the passage.

**The business of collecting, though governed by the laws of supply and demand, is very complicated, because the star quality of the player has to be factored in.**

Where could the sentence best fit?

看看文章裡四個字母，哪個地方可以把下面句子安插進去

雖然一樣受供需法則支配，但是收集卡片這種生意非常複雜，因為球員的明星素質必須列入考量因素。

這句子放哪裡最合適？

### 解析

答案｜(A)

❶ 這一句話沒有代名詞、沒有指示詞、沒有轉折語，關鍵形容詞、關鍵名詞全部空空如也，可說是要什麼沒什麼，但還有最後一個保命招數－檢視一下題目這句話是不是這個段落的主題句？

❷ 主題句是將整個段落的精華濃縮成一兩句，再瀏覽整個段落驗證一下，只要是正牌主題句，整個段落幾乎所有句子再怎麼翻轉、再怎麼變化，都不會脫離主旨。

❸ 題目句子大意是：棒球卡背後有一套複雜的生意經，尤其是不能遺漏球員未來的發展潛力，確實有君臨天下的架勢。整段文章內容則是名人堂、強打者、投手⋯⋯都不脫它的範圍，答案果真是 (A) 沒錯。

## ⚙ 深度應用分析：對付閱讀就是要化「繁」為「簡」。先刪去( )、[ ] 內的文字，找出主要的主詞和動詞！

❶ (The business of collecting, though governed by the laws of supply and demand, is very complicated), because (the star quality of the player has to be factored in).

### 👈 解析

❶ because 連接兩句。前面這一句是分詞構句，原來應該是以下兩句：

Though the business of collecting is governed by the laws of supply and demand.

The business of collecting is very complicated.

因為主詞都是 the business of collecting，所以省略掉。雖然連接詞 though 也可以省略掉，但是為了避免語意不清，還是保留下來。值得注意的是，這種情況不適用於 because、as，也就是說表原因的連接詞一定要省略。例如：

Animals can do many amazing things if properly trained.

（假如好好訓練，動物也能做出許多驚人的事。）

When asked what to do, she was at a loss.

（當被問到怎麼辦時，她茫然不知所措。）

❷ (Once the pastime of grade school kids) and (originally a simple hobby with few rules), collecting baseball cards has become big business, and gleeful hobbyists have been transfigured into serious-minded investors.

🖛 解析

❶ Once the pastime of grade school kids 和 originally a simple hobby with few rules 都是 collecting baseball cards 的同位語。

❷ 介系詞 into 可以表示變化的結果，所以通常跟 turn、change、convert、transform、transfigure、translate、divide、separate、sort…動詞連用，表示由 A 狀態變為 B 狀態，例如：

The teacher divided the students into six groups.

（老師把學生分成六個小組。）

My boss asked me to translate this passage into Chinese.

（我的老闆要我把這篇文章翻成中文。）

單元 1

單元 2

單元 3

單元 4

從拆解藝術、人文類題目，看分詞構句、介系詞的角色

單元 5

單元 6

# The Art of Horace Pippin (1)

## 小人物大畫作（1）

 閱讀原文：試用 **3** 分鐘的時間念完文章，記得先把中文遮上，並翻頁看題目問什麼。計時開始！

### The Art of Horace Pippin (1)

During the 1930s, it was unlikely that a middle-aged African American from a small town in Pennsylvania would achieve success as a painter, including the fact that the man had never studied art, had earned his living as a hotel porter and used-clothes **peddler**, and had all but lost the use of his right arm. Horace Pippin had one of the most implausible careers in the history of twentieth-century art.

Born into a family just one generation removed from slavery, Pippin joined the army in 1917 at the age of twenty-nine. In Europe during World War I, he was shot by a **sniper**. As **therapy** for his injured arm, he started decorating discarded cigar boxes, **whittling** picture frames, and burning images on wood **panels** with a hot **poker**. It wasn't until 1930 that he tried oil painting for the first time, **propping** up his right arm with his left hand. The subject of Horace Pippin's earliest paintings is World War I. What is most interesting concerning these early efforts is the three-dimensional effect of hundreds of layers of paint.

## 小人物大畫作（1）

1930 年代來自賓州一個小鎮的中年黑人竟然可以在畫壇闖出一片天根本是癡人說夢，這還包含以下事實：這人從來沒學過美術，靠著在旅館打雜、叫賣二手衣服餬口，右手幾乎失去功用。在二十世紀藝術史裡，何瑞斯·匹平的生涯可說是最難以置信的其中一個。

匹平出生於上一代才剛擺脫黑奴身分的家庭，1917 年 29 歲從軍，在第一次世界大戰歐洲戰場中被狙擊手射傷。為了給患肢做物理治療，他開始拿廢棄的香菸盒加以修飾，削整圖框，用炙熱的火鉤在木頭面板上燒出圖像。一直到 1930 年他才第一次畫油畫，還是用左手托住右手來作畫。匹平最早的畫作主題是第一次世界大戰，這些早期傑作很有意思的地方是幾百層顏料形成的立體效果。

**Which of the following is NOT the reason the author refers to Horace Pippin's career as implausible?**

(A) As a descendent of slaves he had a very low social status.

(B) He was physically challenged.

(C) He did not receive any professional training for an artist.

(D) Many of his early works deal with World War I.

作者認為何瑞斯·匹平的生涯難以置信，其原因不包含以下哪一點？

(A) 身為奴隸的子孫，他社會地位卑下

(B) 他肢體殘障

(C) 他並非藝術科班出身

(D) 他許多早期作品都是關於的一次世界大戰

👉 解析

答案 | (D)

❶ 要是不懂 implausible，這一題就要吃虧了。implausible 可能把你考倒了，但是 applause、applaud「鼓掌」總不至於吧！以下透過 applaud 的深層剖析，讓 implausible 在你腦

海裡生根，再也忘不了：

applaud = ap(to) + plaud(plaudit)

plaudit 即「鼓掌、稱讚」，所以 applaud 照字面解讀是「對……鼓掌」。什麼時候會鼓掌？當然是演講人說得很棒，或者演員演得很像，可以給予掌聲鼓勵，這就叫 plausible「似乎有道理的、貌似真實的」。再加上表示否定的字首 im-就成為 implausible「難以置信的、不像真實的」。換句話說，Horace Pippin 條件那麼糟糕，中年因緣際會居然還能在藝術領域大放異彩，這樣的傳奇人生簡直是小說、電影裡才會有的情節，不像是真人實事。

❷ 解題關鍵是第一句…including the fact that…後面的同位語子句，這子句點出 Horace Pippin 非凡之處

(1) He had never studied art. 即選項 (C)。

(2) He had earned his living as a hotel porter and used-clothes peddler. 即選項 (A)。

(3) He had all but lost the use of his right arm. 即選項 (B)。

(4) (D) 是孤兒，因此答案就是它。

## 深度應用分析：對付閱讀就是要化「繁」為「簡」。先刪去( )、[ ] 內的文字，找出主要的主詞和動詞！

❶ During the 1930s, it was unlikely that a middle-aged African American (from a small town in Pennsylvania) would achieve success as a painter, including the fact [that the man had never studied art, had earned his living as a hotel porter and used-clothes peddler, and had all but lost the use of his right arm].

### 解析

❶ 小括號裡面的 from a small town in Pennsylvania 修飾前面的 a middle-aged African American。中括號裡面的 that 子句是 the fact 的同位語，説明這個黑人不單單中年轉換跑道，在美術界闖出名堂而已，以下這三點更是叫人跌破眼鏡。

❷ including 是現在分詞轉化來的介系詞，文法上叫做「分詞介系詞」，類似的介系詞還有 excluding「除了…之外、不包括」、concerning「關於」、regarding「關於」、respecting「關於」、considering「就……而論」。例如：Considering his young age, he is very mature and responsible. （以他這麼輕的年紀來說，他很成熟而且盡責。）

❷ Born into a family (just one generation removed from slavery), Pippin joined the army in 1917 at the age of twenty-nine.

👉 解析

❶ 這句話由以下兩句構成

Pippin was born into a family just one generation removed from slavery.

Pippin joined the army in 1917 at the age of twenty-nine.

兩句主詞都是 Pippin，所以省略掉；單憑過去分詞 born 就足以表達被動涵義，所以 be 動詞也省略。括號框起來的 just one generation removed from slavery 修飾 a family。

❷ 1917 年 Pippin29 歲當兵，這是很重要的訊息，因為從這句話可以反推 Pippin 出生於 1888 年（**注意：中文認為人一出生是 1 歲，但是英文卻認為是 0 歲，必須到隔年才是 1 歲。**）。結合本文倒數第二句 It wasn't until 1930 that he tried oil painting for the first time…可以得知 1930 年 Pippin 開始畫油畫，那一年 42 歲。

從拆解藝術、人文類題目，看分詞構句、介系詞的角色

# The Art of Horace Pippin (2)

# 小人物大畫作（2）

💡 閱讀原文：試用 3 分鐘的時間念完文章，記得先把中文遮上，並翻頁看題目問什麼。計時開始！

### The Art of Horace Pippin (2)

Pippin's representations of African American life are considered the **apogee** of his achievements as a painter attentive to popular culture. **Culling** images from magazines, films, and illustrated calendars, he committed **vignettes** of family life and seasonal activities to wood panels from doors, tables, or furniture cases. Often the **varnish** on the original surface provided the principal coloring. A humble charm **suffuses** these memorable scenes, alive with detail down to each lacy edge of a **doily** and every braid of a rag rug.

In 1937, Horace Pippin's paintings came to the attention of an art critic, who encouraged him to contribute several works to an art show outside of Philadelphia. His paintings were so well received that for a time, Pippin was more famous than Grandma Moses, with **tributes** from coast to coast and works reproduced in all the major magazines. Unfortunately, his fame was **transient**. He died in 1946, having completed 140 paintings, drawings, and wood panels. In his short but extraordinary career, this self-taught painter **exalted** the commonplace and commemorated his unique vision of history, nature, and people.

## 小人物大畫作（2）

　　身為一位留意流行文化的畫家，匹平對非裔美國人生活的呈現被視為成就的巔峰。他從雜誌、電影、月曆中擷取圖像，把家庭生活、季節活動的小插圖套進從門、桌子、家具箱拆下來的木框裡，往往拿原來表面的顏料來當主要色調。這值得懷念的場景裡瀰漫著一股簡樸的魅力，連一塊桌巾每個蕾絲邊、一塊碎布地毯的每個穗帶這些細節都活靈活現。


　　1937 年匹平的畫引起一位美術評論家的注意，勸他把一些作品捐給賓州外面的一個畫展展覽。匹平畫作接受度高到有一陣子名氣甚至都比摩西奶奶還響亮，不只在美國傳頌一時，各大雜誌也廣為翻印其作品。很不幸的是，他的人氣有如曇花一現。1946 年他過世了，總共完成 140 幅畫作、木製圖框。在他短暫

卻不凡的一生中，這位無師自通的畫家提升了市井小民的層次，讓他對歷史、自然、人類獨到的觀察走入世人的記憶裡。

 考題演練及解析

**Which of the following best expresses the essential information in the underlined sentence? Incorrect answer choices change the meaning in important ways or leave out essential information.**

(A) When Horace Pippin passed away at the age of 58, his total output comprised only about 140 pieces of artwork.

(B) In 1946 Horace Pippin died a prolific painter.

(C) Though Horace Pippin demised in 1946, a number of his works have been finished recently.

(D) When Horace Pippin deceased, there were still 140 of his creations yet to be completed.

以下哪一句最能表達出劃底線句子的基本訊息？不正確的答案選項會以重要方式改變句義，或者遺漏基本訊息

(A) 匹平 58 歲過世時，他全部作品才 140 幅而已。

(B) 1946 年匹平過世時已經是一位多產的畫家。

(C) 雖然匹平在 1946 年過世，許多他的作品最近才剛完成。

(D) 匹平 1946 年往生時，還有 140 幅作品有待完成。

## 👉 解析

答案｜**(A)**

❶ 前一篇文章說 1917 年 Pippin29 歲當兵，從這個訊息可以反推 Pippin 出生於 1888 年。1946 年逝世時正好 58 歲，所以答案是 (A)。

❷ (B) 選項的 prolific = proli(proles) + fic(make、do)。

這字由兩個字根組成。前面字根即 proles「子嗣」，這是集合名詞，單數 prole 是「窮人」。窮人怎麼會牽扯上子嗣呢？原來古羅馬帝國那些社會最底層的百姓不只繳不起稅，每天忙著張羅三餐也無暇服役，對社會唯一的貢獻是增產報國延續香火，為國家提供男丁。prole 這麼冷僻的字眼恐怕過眼即忘，但是你對「普羅大眾」、「普羅文學」這些名詞應該不陌生吧！所謂「普羅」其實就是 prole 音譯而來。後來共產主義興起以後，家無恆產、一窮二白的 proletariat「無產階級」更是飛上枝頭變鳳凰。

prolific 從字根來看，頗有努力作人的感覺，因此是「多產的」。Horace Pippin 一生作品才 140 件，叫 prolific 實在太沉重！

從拆解藝術、人文類題目，看分詞構句、介系詞的角色

## ⚙ 深度應用分析：對付閱讀就是要化「繁」為「簡」。先刪去( )、[ ] 內的文字，找出主要的主詞和動詞！

**❶** He died in 1946, having completed 140 paintings, drawings, and wood panels.

### 👉 解析

**❶** 這句話由以下兩句構成：

He died in 1946.

He had completed 140 paintings, drawings, and wood panels.

兩句發生時間不一樣，當然是先完成 140 幅作品，然後再過世。合併的方法大致都和普通分詞構句相同，先將副詞子句的主詞省略掉。但是為避免讀者將兩個句子發生先後順序搞混，所以把先發生的動作，也就是副詞子句中完成式的 have/has/had 改為 having。

❷ His paintings were so well received that for a time, Pippin was more famous than Grandma Moses, [with tributes (from coast to coast) and works(reproduced in all the major magazines)].

👉 **解析**

❶ 小括號框起來的 from coast to coast 修飾 tributes，從美國東岸到西岸，所以就是橫越整個美洲大陸，到處都在歌頌。另一個小括號框起來的 reproduced in all the major magazines 修飾 works。

❷ 這個句子主要由以下兩個部分構成————

- His paintings were well received.
- For a time, Pippin was more famous than Grandma Moses, with tributes from coast to coast and works reproduced in all the major magazines. 兩句用 so…that…表示結果的句型合併。最後 His works were reproduced in all the major magazines 的 His 和 were 也在不影響句意的條件下省略了。

# Blue Jeans: From Miners' Wear to American Classic (1)

## 牛仔褲：從礦工穿著到美國經典（1）

💡 閱讀原文：試用 3 分鐘的時間念完文章，記得先把中文遮上，並翻頁看題目問什麼。計時開始！

**Blue Jeans: From Miners' Wear to American Classic (1)**

Well over 600 million pairs were sold in 1992 alone, making jeans the best-selling pants in the world. Throughout their **hallowed** history, jeans have never gone out of style. Blue jeans got their name long before they reached their current popularity. In the late sixteenth century, the cotton cloth used to make them was called Genoa Fustian after Genoa, Italy, where the material was first woven. Genoa, with Fustian dropped, was changed to Gene and then to Jean by the English, and the work pants made from the material were called blue jeans for their color.

The first pair of jeans were made by Levi Strauss, a

Bavarian **immigrant** to the United States. In 1850, Strauss went to California with **bolts** of brown canvas that he hoped to sell as tenting to gold miners. When he realized how quickly miners' work clothes wore out, he decided to use the canvas to make **staunch** pants. Having used up his canvas stock, he ordered a type of thick strong cotton cloth called denim from a **textile** manufacturer in New Hampshire.

## 牛仔褲：從礦工穿著到美國經典（1）

　　單單 1992 年就賣出 6 億多件，讓牛仔褲成為世界上最熱賣的褲子。綜觀其不凡的歷史，牛仔褲從來不曾退過流行。牛仔褲得名遠在今天風行於世之前。在十六世紀晚期，用來製作牛仔褲的棉布叫做 Genoa Fustian「熱內亞粗斜條棉布」，以義大利熱內亞這地方來命名，因為這種布料最早是在那裡編織的。Fustian 先消失掉，Genoa 變成 Gene，然後英國人再將它拼成 Jean，這種布料作成的工作褲因為顏色的緣故所以叫做 blue jeans。

　　第一件牛仔褲是李維·史特勞斯製作的，他從巴伐利亞移民到美國。1850 年他帶著好幾疋棕色帆布到加州，原本希望賣給淘金礦工當帳篷。當他得悉礦工的工作衣褲磨損得很快時，便決定用這些帆布來縫製結實的褲子。把帆布庫存用完後，他只好跟新罕布夏一家紡織公司訂購厚重但是用途更廣的布料，這種布料

從拆解藝術、人文類題目，看分詞構句、介系詞的角色

就叫丁尼布。

## 考題演練及解析

**Where did the word "jeans" come from?**

(A) A Bavarian immigrant

(B) A dyed color

(C) A girl's name

(D) An Italian city

「**jeans**」這個字源自何處？

(A) 一位巴伐利亞移民。

(B) 一種染出來的顏色。

(C) 一個女孩子的名字。

(D) 一個義大利城市。

 解析

答案｜(D)

❶ jeans 字形演變堪稱英文的變形金剛，從英文拼字 jeans 很難看得出來它源自義大利熱內亞 Genoa 這個地名。解說最詳盡的莫過於第一段最後一句 Genoa, with Fustian dropped, …，從這句話可以知道：

(1) jeans 最早的稱呼是 Genoa Fustian「熱內亞粗斜條棉布」。

(2) 然後 Fustian 不見了，只剩下 Genoa，彷彿我們把「電動玩具」省略成「電動」一樣。

(3) 之後 Genoa 拼字出現更動，改拼成 Gene，注意這個 Gene 跟 gene「基因」只是碰巧拼字相同，彼此血緣關係井水不犯河水。彷彿中文「肉」當部首時會寫成「月」，但是實際上跟月亮一點關係也沒有。

(4) 傳進英文以後，Gene 改頭換面成為 Jean，一樣要注意這個 Jean 跟女孩名字 Jean 也是碰巧拼字相同，彼此毫無任何瓜葛。

(5) 因為英文衣褲幾乎都視為複數，再加上牛仔褲往往染成不怕髒的藍色，我們熟悉的 blue jeans 至此總算變身成功。

❷ 整個流程九拐十八彎，但是還是不能轉昏頭，jeans 最早還是源自 Genoa 這個地名，所以答案是 (D)。

## ⚙️ 深度應用分析：對付閱讀就是要化「繁」為「簡」。先刪去( )、[ ] 內的文字，找出主要的主詞和動詞！

❶ [Genoa, with Fustian dropped, was changed to Gene and then to Jean by the English], and [the work pants (made from the material) were called blue jeans for their color].

### 👉 解析

❶ and 連接兩句。後面那句小括號框起來的 made from the material 是要修飾 the work pants。

❷ 前面這一句是分詞構句，原先應該是這樣：

Fustian was dropped and Genoa was changed to Gene and then to Jean by the English.

因為主詞不一樣，所以 Fustian 要保留下來。was 改成 being，可是單憑過去分詞 dropped 就能表達被動，所以 being 省略。再加上表示附帶狀況的介系詞 with，強調這是伴隨發生的動作或狀態，也就是說就在 Genoa 改拼成 Gene 時，Fustian 也消失掉了。

❷ Having used up his canvas stock, he ordered a type of thick strong cotton cloth (called denim) from a textile manufacturer in New Hampshire.

## ☞ 解析

❶ 這句話原本是這樣：

Because he used up his canvas stock, he ordered a type of thick strong cotton cloth called denim from a textile manufacturer in New Hampshire.

因為主詞都是 he，所以主詞和連接詞 Because 都省略掉。為避免讀者搞錯時間先後順序，所以保留原來完成式的模樣，只把 had 改成 Having。

❷ 小括號裡的 called denim 修飾前面的 a type of thick strong cotton cloth。

從拆解藝術、人文類題目，看分詞構句、介系詞的角色

Ch 1

Ch 2

Ch 3

Ch 4

Ch 5

Ch 6

**Blue Jeans: From Miners' Wear to American Classic (2)**

牛仔褲：從礦工穿著到美國經典（2）

**Blue Jeans: From Miners' Wear to American Classic (2)**

(A) Strauss's pants were enormously popular with the miners, with one exception: the pockets tore off too easily when the men filled them with **lumps** of **ore**. (B) Some **extrinsic** modifications followed, such as the "bird in flight" **stitching** on the back pockets. (C)

Although we take them for granted now, jeans were not widely accepted until the late 1970s. (D) Designer jeans were the rage in the 1980s, when **stonewashed** and faded denim were introduced for those who had no time to let their jeans age gracefully. More **gratuitous** innovations were **inaugurated**, such as zippers up and down the pants legs, fashionable patches in strategic places, and carefully designed machine rips and tears.

In spite of all the **fine-tuning**, basic blue jeans not only have survived, but they have triumphed. People from around the world **covet** jeans as pieces of Americana that rank with Mickey Mouse and fast food. Recycled jeans are a hot **commodity**, often selling overseas at five times their original price.

## 牛仔褲：從礦工穿著到美國經典（2）

（A）史特勞斯的褲子受到礦工的盛大歡迎，可惜有一個例外：當人們在口袋塞滿一塊塊礦石時，口袋很容易裂開來。（B）之後又修改過外表，例如在背後口袋繡上「飛鳥」圖案。（C）

雖然現在我們把牛仔褲視為家常便飯，但是要到 1970 年代晚期才廣為接受。（D）標名牛仔褲在 1980 年代成為時尚，那時還為那些沒時間讓牛仔褲老舊得很優雅的人，特地引入砂洗與褪色丁尼布。還進行更多五花八門的創新，像是在褲管加上拉鍊，在重要部位加上新潮補丁，精心設計的機械裂縫與破洞。

儘管有這些調整，陽春牛仔褲不只存活下來，甚至還發揚光大。全世界的人都喜歡牛仔褲，將之視為美國文化的一部分，與米老鼠和速食齊名。回收牛仔褲也是一種熱門商品，常常以原價五倍的價格賣到國外去。

Look at the four letters that indicate where the following sentence could be added to the passage.

**Such being the case, in 1873 he added the copper rivets that strengthen the pocket seams.**

Where could the sentence best fit?

看看文章裡四個字母,哪個地方可以把下面句子安插進去

既然是這種情況,1873 年他加上可以強化口袋縫線的銅製鉚釘。

這句子放哪裡最合適?

👉 解析

答案 | (B)

❶ 作插入句題型時,要設法從題目句子儘可能解讀出隱藏的訊息。從這句子應該要看出以下端倪:

(1) 既然句子提到 1873 年,但是 (D) 卻排在 1970 年末期,所以答案不會是 (D)。

(2) 一開頭天上就掉下兩個大餡餅:指示詞 Such 和關鍵名詞 the case。這兩個線索暗示前面一定有提到某個情況。

(3) 另外那一句話又說 he added the copper rivets that

strengthen the pocket seams 又砸下一大餡餅— 代名詞 he。沒猜錯的話,應該是指 Strauss,因為整篇文章就只提到他。代名詞一般都不會離所代替的名詞太遠,因為假如中間夾雜太多名詞,很容易讓讀者混淆。

(4) 分析另外這句話發現牛仔褲加上可以強化口袋縫線的銅製鉚釘,配合前面的 Such being the case,可以判斷某個問題似乎因此解決了。

❷ 綜合上述四點,很快就能發現 (B) 最理想,因為第一句話就提到一個大毛病 the pockets tore off too easily,還出現 Strauss 為題目句的 he 鋪好路。緊接後面的 Some extrinsic modifications followed⋯又提到外部繼續作了一些修改。

*Unit 1*

*Unit 2*

*Unit 3*

*Unit 4*

從拆解藝術、人文類題目,看分詞構句、介系詞的角色

*Unit 5*

*Unit 6*

⚙ **深度應用分析：對付閱讀就是要化「繁」為「簡」。先刪去( )、[] 內的文字，找出主要的主詞和動詞！**

❶ Such being the case, in 1873 he added the copper rivets(that strengthen the pocket seams).

👉 **解析**

❶ 還記得 Ch3 3-6 Icarus and Daedalus (2) 介紹過一個準關係代名詞的句型嗎？As was the case with wayward children…這句話的分詞構句部分其實就是上述句型，原來句型應該是 Such is the case (with …)，意思是「……情況也是這樣」。

❷ 題目這句話是獨立分詞構句，原來應該是這樣：
Because such was the case, in 1873 he added the copper rivets that strengthen the pocket seams.
兩句主詞不一樣，所以 such 保留下來，只省略連接詞 Because。was 改成現在分詞 being。可以把 Such being the case 視為分詞慣用語使用，意思是「既然情況如此」。

❸ that strengthen the pocket seams 修飾前面的 the copper rivets。

❷ Designer jeans were the rage in the 1980s, [when stonewashed and faded denim were introduced for those (who had no time to let their jeans age gracefully)].

### 解析

❶ those 後面有 people 省略掉了，小括號框起來的 who had no time to let their jeans age gracefully 修飾 those people。

❷ 關係副詞 when，意思乃「那時候」，先行詞是逗點前面的 the 1980s，所引領的附屬子句主詞是 stonewashed and faded denim，were introduced 表被動。

❸ stonewashed、faded 都是表示被動的過去分詞，當形容詞修飾後面的 denim，表示那些丁尼布料是經過人們砂洗到褪色的狀態。

❹ rage 來自一個迷你家族，核心意思是「狂」。rabies「狂犬病」。注意有的字尾-s 意思是「病」，千萬不能將之視為複數，例如：measles「麻疹」、mumps「腮腺炎」。rabid「激烈的、瘋狂的」是 rabies 的形容詞；outrageous = out(beyond) + rage + ous(形容詞字尾)，超出瘋狂的程度，所以是「暴虐的、不尋常的」rage 一般都做「狂怒」解，但是在此句是指「令大家瘋狂著迷的事物」，等於 fashion、fad。

*Unit* 1

*Unit* 2

*Unit* 3

*Unit* 4

*Unit* 5

*Unit* 6

從拆解藝術、人文類題目，看分詞構句、介系詞的角色

# Unit 5-1

## Harriet Tubman (1)

### 哈瑞特・塔曼（1）

閱讀原文：試用 **3** 分鐘的時間念完文章，記得先把中文遮上，並翻頁看題目問什麼。計時開始！

### Harriet Tubman (1)

Born a slave in Maryland around 1815, Harriet Tubman was forced to work as a field hand by her cruel **plantation** overseer. Driven by the belief that all African Americans should be free, Tubman fled the plantation in 1849, leaving behind her husband, her parents, and her brothers and sisters. Her **unequivocal** dedication to this cause never wavered.

Risking her life as well as her freedom, she returned to the South no fewer than 19 times to lead her family and hundreds of other slaves to freedom. Tubman guided the escaping slaves north along the Underground Railroad, a secret organization that aided the escape of slaves to

Canada. None of the **fugitives** Harriet Tubman led to safety was ever captured. All the while, Tubman herself was pursued by **bounty** hunters who sought the 40 thousand dollars offered for her capture. Tubman later **conspired** with John Brown when he planned his attack on Harper's Ferry in 1858. Tubman provided valuable information that helped him carry out his **raid** in which she even planned to participate but was ill at the time.

## 哈瑞特・塔曼（1）

　　在 1815 年馬里蘭州，哈瑞特·塔曼一生下來就是黑奴，因此在殘酷的農莊管家淫威下被迫成為農場勞工。在所有黑人都應該自由的信念驅使下，1849 年塔曼留下丈夫、父母、手足，隻身逃離農莊，對這明確的信念矢志不渝，從未動搖。

　　她賭上自己身家性命與自由，潛回南方不下 19 次，帶領家人和成百上千名其他黑奴逃向自由。塔曼引導著跑路的黑奴在奴隸援助秘密組織「地下鐵道」的掩護下逃向加拿大。塔曼帶領下的黑奴逃犯沒有半個被逮。這段期間塔曼自己也被懸賞四萬塊，一票垂涎賞金的鷹犬緊咬著她不放。後來 1858 年約翰布朗計畫攻擊哈普渡口時，塔曼和他密謀大計，提供有助於突襲的寶貴情報。本來她還打算參與這次突襲，但是當時卻病倒了。

**Which of the following best expresses the essential information in the underlined sentence? Incorrect answer choices change the meaning in important ways or leave out essential information.**

(A) Tubman's firm belief in freedom for all blacks encouraged her to leave the fields alone in secret.

(B) As an African American, Tubman abandoned her family members to escape slavery.

(C) Tubman ran away from her owner, believing that all African Americans in the North had been emancipated from slavery.

(D) Convinced that all black people should be free, Tubman was driven out of the farms.

以下哪一句最能表達出劃底線句子的基本訊息？不正確的答案選項會以重要方式改變句義，或者遺漏基本訊息

(A) 塔曼對解放黑人的堅定信念鼓舞著她隻身偷偷逃離農場。

(B) 身為黑人，塔曼為了擺脫奴隸處境，只好拋棄家人。

(C) 塔曼深信所有北方黑人都已獲得解放，所以逃出主人魔掌。

(D) 塔曼深信黑人都應該自由，所以被趕出農場。

### 解析

答案｜**(A)**

❶ 句構重述題解題時，不能像一般閱讀測驗，單憑語意敘述無誤，直接就作答。假如是這樣土法煉鋼，碰到 TOEFL 句構重述題一定會傻眼，因為有時考題會出現四個選項語意描述都正確的情況。

❷ 萬一碰到很刁鑽的句構重述題，還是要回頭把題目看得一清二楚。句構重述題的題目永遠都是千篇一律，其中 Which of the following best expresses the essential information in the underlined sentence?是老掉牙的問題模式，不足為奇。後面提醒 incorrect answer choices 會有兩種情況，第一種是 change the meaning in important ways，因為會改變語意，所以還好應付，但是要搞清楚整個句子是哪一種邏輯關係，以及用字上些微的差異；第二個是 leave out essential information，這個就比較棘手一點，因為這種選項語意一定正確，只是它所描述的是枝節末梢，卻把重要的主幹遺漏掉。

❸ (B) 選項是標準 leave out essential information 的情況；(C) (D) 選項則是 change the meaning in important ways；因此答案是 (A)。

從拆解歷史類題目，看看補述用法的角色

❶ Driven by the belief (that all African Americans should be free), Tubman fled the plantation in 1849, (leaving behind her husband, her parents, and her brothers and sisters).

👉 解析

❶ that all African Americans should be free 是 the belief 的同位語，補充説明 Tubman 抱持著所有黑人都應該獲得自由的信念，就是在這信念的驅使下逃向自由。

❷ 同位語是補述用法的一種，補語也是補述用法的一種，但是二者不能混為一談。補語是句法結構的一部分，不能刪除，否則會造成語意不完整；同位語只是針對名詞作補充説明，即使刪掉，也不會造成語法錯誤。補語只會出現在連綴動詞、感官動詞、使役動詞後面，常常是名詞或形容詞；但是同位語則往往緊接在名詞（片語／子句）後面，常常也是名詞（片語／子句）。

❸ 這個 that 是連接詞，而且不能省略。同位語的 that 跟關係代名詞的 that 同樣不能混為一談。

❹ 分詞片語 leaving behind her husband, her parents, and her brothers and sisters 說明 Tubman 暫時拋棄所有親屬獨自一人逃離農場。

❷ Born a slave in Maryland around 1815, Harriet Tubman was forced to work as a field hand by her cruel plantation overseer.

### 👉 解析

❶ 英文少數表動作和過程的動詞，雖然不是連綴動詞，但是後面也可以接補語修飾主詞，例如：arrive、escape、stand、sit、lie、die、survive、be born、grow up⋯

She **arrived** unannounced at my door.

（她沒打聲招呼，人就到我家門前了。）

He **returned** home a changed man.

（他回家時已經改頭換面了。）

She **married** young but her husband died young.

（她早婚，但老公卻英年早逝。）

He **escaped** unhurt.

（他毫髮無損逃脫了。）

She **lay** awake thinking about her future.

（她清醒躺著思考著自己未來。）

**Born** a slave in Maryland around 1815 意味 1815 年 Tubman 出生時，身分就是黑奴。

💡 閱讀原文：試用 3 分鐘的時間念完文章，記得先
把中文遮上，並翻頁看題目問什麼。計時開始！

### Harriet Tubman (2)

(A) When the Civil War broke out three years later, Tubman assisted the Union Army as a nurse and served as both a scout and a spy. (B) She was so important to the Union Army that she was a leader of a **corps** of local blacks who ventured into rebel **territory** to gather information. (C) Because she was privy to information on the location of warehouses and **ammunition depots**, she was able to provide Union commanders with vital information, some of which helped Colonel James Montgomery make several **expeditions** into southern areas to destroy supplies. (D)

After the war, Tubman returned to New York, where,

while caring for her own family, she helped escaped and newly freed blacks begin their lives. She earned money by giving speeches and selling copies of her biography. Called "the Moses of her people," Tubman came to personify the strength and determination that eventually led to the civil rights movement of the 1960s.

## 哈瑞特・塔曼（2）

(A) 三年後南北戰爭爆發時，塔曼以護士身分協助同盟軍，擔任斥候、間諜。(B) 她對同盟軍極為重要，擔任當地黑人軍隊的隊長，這支軍隊必須冒險潛入叛軍領域收集情報。(C) 因為她對倉庫與彈藥庫位置的情報嫻熟於心，所以可以提供聯盟軍指揮官重要訊息，其中有些還協助了詹姆士・蒙哥馬利上校冒險深入南方切斷補給線。(D)

戰後塔曼回到紐約，在那裏除了照顧自己家人外，她還協助成功逃跑剛獲得自由的黑人展開新生活。她靠著演講和販賣自傳賺錢。塔曼被稱呼為『黑人的摩西』，展露出力量與決心，最後引發 1960 年代的公民權利運動。

Look at the four letters that indicate where the following sentence could be added to the passage.

**Her knowledge of the land, her experience at secret travel, and her unremarkable looks – Tubman's characters allowed her to carry out her duties without being spotted.**

Where could the sentence best fit?

看看文章裡四個字母，哪個地方可以把下面句子安插進去

對地理風土的了解、暗行訪查的經驗、貌不驚人的外表───塔曼的特質讓她可以執行任務而不被察覺

這句子放哪裡最合適？

🖐 解析

答案│(B)

❶ 雖然題目這句話沒有代名詞、指示詞、關鍵名詞、關鍵形容詞，但是後半部的 these allowed her to carry out her duties without being spotted 卻提供極為重要的線索，加上前半部這三點，可以約略猜出這似乎是擔任偵探、間諜的工作。一個社會地位不高的黑奴怎麼會牽扯上偵探、間諜呢？可是回頭想想上一篇最後一句話 Tubman provided valuable information that helped him carry out his raid in which she even planned to participate but was ill at the time，provided valuable information 這三個字就足以為證。

❷ 另一方面，上一篇文章 Tubman fled the plantation in 1849 這句話又提供一條線索，因為這一年離美國南北戰爭（1861~1865）並不遠。透過這兩個線索可以合理假設 Tubman 在南北戰爭時擔任北軍的間諜。

❸ 開始看本篇文章，開門見山就是 When the Civil War broke out three years later，尤其是後面緊接又說 Tubman assisted the Union Army as a nurse and served as both a scout and a spy，完全印證先前的推測。很快可以發現 (B) 這位置最適合。

❹ (C) 選項位於…she was a leader of a corps of local blacks who ventured into rebel territory to gather information 和…she was able to provide Union commanders with vital information, some of which helped Colonel James Montgomery make several expeditions into southern areas to destroy supplies 這兩個訊息之中，而這兩句都論及南北戰爭的細節。假如把題目句插入其中，顯然會破壞敘述的連貫性，所以 (C) 沒有 (B) 來得流暢。

**深度應用分析：對付閱讀就是要化「繁」為「簡」。先刪去( )、[ ] 內的文字，找出主要的主詞和動詞！**

❶ (Her knowledge of the land), (her experience at secret travel), and (her unremarkable looks) – Tubman's characters allowed her to carry out her duties without being spotted.

**☞ 解析**

❶ 破折號前面三個小括號框起來的 her knowledge of the land、her experience at secret travel、her unremarkable looks 是後面 Tubman's characters 的同位語，也就是這三個特質讓 Tubman 可以安全地潛伏執行任務。

❷ 這句型前半部有許多同位語組成，這些同位語可說是一件事物的多種層面，因此破折號後面必須有一個完整句子做總結，而且其主詞必須能概括前面所有同位語。例如：
An old paragraph, a haunting fragrance, a sudden view of a long-forgotten scene –something sentimental unexpectedly triggers our nostalgia for the past.
（一張老照片、一縷魂牽夢縈的香氣、一幕幕早已遺忘的往事驀然一瞥──觸景生情的事物意外激發了我們的思古幽情。）

❶ Because she was privy to information on the location of warehouses and ammunition depots, she was able to provide Union commanders with vital information, (some of which helped Colonel James Montgomery make several expeditions into southern areas to destroy supplies).

### 👉 解析

❶ 連接詞 because 連接中括號框起來的兩個句子。小括號裡的 some of which 帶領關係子句修飾先行詞 vital information。

❷ 後半部…she was able to provide Union commanders with vital information, some of which helped Colonel James Montgomery make several expeditions into southern areas to destroy supplies 是由以下兩句構成──

● She was able to provide Union commanders with vital information.

● Some of the vital information helped Colonel James Montgomery make several expeditions into southern areas to destroy supplies. 以兩句的交集 vital information 作先行詞，用關係代名詞 which 合併。

*th* 1

*th* 2

*th* 3

*th* 4

*th* 5

從拆解歷史類題目，看看補述用法的角色

*th* 6

# Matthew Henson: With Peary to the Pole (1)

## 馬修 · 韓森：叫我北極第一名（1）

💡 閱讀原文：試用 **3** 分鐘的時間念完文章，記得先把中文遮上，並翻頁看題目問什麼。計時開始！

### Matthew Henson: With Peary to the Pole (1)

Matthew Henson, best known as the co-discoverer of the North Pole with Robert Edwin Peary, was born in 1866 to sharecroppers who had been free people of color before the American Civil War. As an African American, Henson had few options for earning a livelihood. At the age of 15 he worked as a cabin boy on a **vessel bound** for France and the Philippines. The ship's captain liked Henson and urged him to utilize the ship's library to learn navigation. Henson studied hard and applied what he learned as the ship traveled from one **exotic** locale to another.

After the captain died, Henson tried to make a life for himself on land, but racial **prejudice** discouraged African

Americans from seeking lofty positions, so Henson took whatever lowly work he was offered, including a job as a stock boy in a naval supply store. That job was a turning point, for it was there that Henson met Peary, a civil engineer for the United States Navy. Henson was **intrigued** by Peary and asked to accompany him on his next voyage.

## 馬修・韓森：叫我北極第一名（1）

馬修·韓森最有名的事蹟是跟羅伯・艾文・派瑞一起發現了北極。1866 年他出生於一戶佃農人家，父母親在南北戰爭前就已經是自由黑人。身為一個黑人，韓森謀生選項少之又少，15 歲時，在一艘前往法國和菲律賓的船上當服務員。船長很喜歡韓森，勸他善用船上圖書館學習航海技術。隨著那艘船在他鄉異國逐一航行，韓森認真學以致用。

船長過世後，韓森想辦法上岸混口飯吃，可是種族歧視使得黑人不敢覬覦高尚一點的職位，所以再怎麼低賤的工作韓森都不能拒絕，這當中包含在海軍用品店當庫存管理員。這工作是他的轉捩點，因為就是在那裏韓森遇見派瑞，那時派瑞還是美國海軍的土木技師。派瑞激起了韓森的興趣，還邀他下次陪同出航。

**The author's description of Matthew Henson mentions which of the following?**

(A) His parents were farmers.

(B) He once served in the Navy.

(C) He was born in a slave family.

(D) He invested in the stock in his childhood.

作者對馬修·韓森的描述有提到以下哪一點？

(A) 他的父母親是農夫

(B) 他曾經在海軍服役

(C) 他出生於黑奴家庭

(D) 童年時期他就玩起股票

### 解析

答案｜(A)

❶ 本題關鍵是開頭第一句。從本句可以知道 Matthew Henson 並非誕生於黑奴家庭，而是自由黑人，因此 (C) 錯誤。此外還能得知父母親是 sharecropper「佃農」，亦即所收成的 crop「農作物」部分必須 share 給 landlord，所以答案是 (A)。

❷ 從本文倒數第二句得知在海軍服役的是 Peary，而非 Henson，因此 (B) 錯誤。

❸ 第二段第一句的 stock 意思是「存貨」，而非「股票」，因此 (D) 也錯誤。

❹ civil「市民的、公民的」跟 city 同源。美國 Civil War 是公民自己人打自己人的內戰，這很好理解。可是「土木工程」怎麼會是 civil engineering 呢？打從人類群居以來，就逐漸形成 city。當初建立 city 需要兩種 engineering：一種是對內民間工程 civil engineering，亦即蓋房子、挖水溝、搭橋樑等；一種是對外軍事工程 military engineering，亦即築城牆、製作武器、後勤補給等。隨著 civilization 愈來愈進步，engineering 分工愈來愈細，electronic engineering、chemical engineering、mechanical engineering…紛紛出籠，但是最初蓋房子、挖水溝、搭橋樑這些人類最早習得的技術還是繼續叫 civil engineering

❶ Matthew Henson, (best known as the co-discoverer of the North Pole with Robert Edwin Peary), was born in 1866 to sharecroppers (who had been free people of color before the American Civil War).

### ☞ 解析

❶ best known as the co-discoverer of the North Pole with Robert Edwin Peary 是 Matthew Henson 的同位語，透過它來補充說明 Matthew Henson 一生最大的成就，讓讀者知道他是何方神聖。這種補述用法在 TOEFL 的閱讀測驗裡不勝枚舉，但是要注意：同位語跟關係代名詞一樣，有先行詞，也有補述用法和限定用法的差異。前者表示同位語為額外補充資訊，若將其刪除也不會影響句意，所以其前後通常使用逗點、括弧、破折號和句子其他部分隔開；後者表示同位語為必要資訊，若將其刪除，將會使其所限定的先行詞的意思變得曖昧不明，所以前面不能有標點符號。例如：

My brother John is an engineer.

（我有好幾個兄弟，叫約翰的才是工程師。）

My brother, John, is an engineer.

（我只有一個兄弟叫約翰，他是工程師。）

❷ 關係子句 who had been free people of color before the American Civil War 的先行詞是 sharecroppers，這是關係代名詞的限定用法。

❷ [After (the captain died), (Henson tried to make a life for himself on land)], but [racial prejudice discouraged African Americans from seeking lofty positions], so [Henson took whatever lowly work (he was offered), including a job as a stock boy in a naval supply store].

👉 **解析**

❶ 這句話長歸長，但是結構並不複雜，最特別的只有 whatever lowly work he was offered 這部分。whatever 是關係形容詞，小括弧框起來的 he was offered 是要修飾 whatever lowly work

❷ **lofty**「高尚的、崇高的」跟 lift「提高、舉起」有關，都是源自 lev 這個字根家族，意思是「舉起」。例如：

**lever**= lev + er(名詞字尾)。字尾-er 即「…東西」，「槓桿」是協助舉起物品的東西。

**levitate** = levit + ate(動詞字尾)，即 lift off「升空、漂浮」。

**elevate** = e(out) + lev + ate(動詞字尾)「舉起、提高」。

# Matthew Henson: With Peary to the Pole (2)

## 馬修‧韓森：叫我北極第一名（2）

🔆 閱讀原文：試用 3 分鐘的時間念完文章，記得先把中文遮上，並翻頁看題目問什麼。計時開始！

### Matthew Henson: With Peary to the Pole (2)

Over the next 20 years, Peary made seven trips to the Arctic. Henson became an invaluable member of Peary's crew, acting mainly as Peary's personal attendant. Henson also learned the Inuit language and helped establish a solid working relationship between the native people of the Arctic **region** and Peary's crew.

It was on the 1908-1909 voyage that Peary decided to locate the North Pole. Since the journey was **arduous**, Peary sent back all the members of his party except for Henson and four Inuit guides. Henson's ability to communicate with the guides in their own language and his knowledge of navigation made him indispensable. Suffering from exhaustion and **frostbite**, Peary left Henson the task of discovering the Pole. On April 6,1909, the former cabin boy became the first person to stand on the North Pole.

While Peary and his crew returned home heroes and were showered with medals and adulation, Henson was left unnoticed and unmentioned until more than 30 years later. In 1944, 11 years before he died, Henson was finally awarded the **Congressional** Medal of Honor.

## 馬修‧韓森：叫我北極第一名（2）

之後 20 年派瑞去北極七趟，韓森也成為派瑞船上不可多得的一員，主要是擔任派瑞的個人助理。韓森還學會伊努特語，協助派瑞船員跟北極地區原住民建立起可靠的工作關係。

就在 1908 到 1909 那次航行，派瑞決心要找出北極的位置。因為這趟旅行極為險惡，派瑞把所有夥伴都資遣了，只離下韓森和四名伊努特嚮導。韓森會用嚮導母語跟他們溝通，也深諳航海技術，這一切都讓他不可或缺。因為派瑞為疲倦與凍傷所苦，就把發現北極的任務交代給韓森。1909 年 4 月 6 日以前幹過服務員的韓森成為第一位駐足北極的人。

派瑞跟他的船員以英雄的姿態光榮歸國，勳章、讚譽紛至沓來，韓森卻慘遭冷落，就這樣持續到 30 多年以後。在韓森過世前 11 年，也就是 1944 年，他終於獲頒國會榮譽勳章。

**Which of the following best expresses the essential information in the underlined sentence? Incorrect answer choices change the meaning in important ways or leave out essential information.**

(A) Triumphant when they returned, Peary received many accolades for his accomplishment, but Henson was pushed out of the limelight.

(B) Still left in the North Pole by the time Peary returned to civilization, Henson stayed there until 1944.

(C) After their return to the States, Peary took all the credit for the incredible accomplishment, but Henson left for the Arctic without being noticed or reported.

(D) Tributes flooded in after their journey back from the Arctic but Henson claimed no personal credit, left, and did not mention their feats until 30 years later.

以下哪一句最能表達出劃底線句子的基本訊息？不正確的答案選項會以重要方式改變句義，或者遺漏基本訊息

(A) 派瑞凱旋歸國，就因非凡成就接受表揚，但是韓森卻無緣吸引鎂光燈。

(B) 派瑞重回文明社會時，韓森還留在北極，就這樣一直待到 1944 年。

(C) 派瑞回到美國以後，這豐功偉業讓派瑞搶盡所有風頭，但是韓森卻在沒人注意與報導的情況下前往北極。

(D) 北極之旅歸來後，各方讚譽蜂擁而至，可是韓森功成不居，轉身而去，直到 30 年後才提及此事。

### 解析

答案 | **(A)**

❶ (A) 選項 limelight 的 **lime** 並非長得很像檸檬的「萊姆」，而是「石灰」，因此 **limelight** 顧名思義就是「灰光燈」。灰光燈是什麼玩意呢？原來石灰說專業一點就是「氧化鈣」，它有一個很重要的特性是用氫氧混合氣火焰加熱會發出強光。電燈發明之前，舞台上都是祭出這一招，另外再加裝透鏡和反射鏡，使它的光線可以聚焦，這就是人類最早的「聚光燈」。一個人只要 in the limelight，那肯定是眾所矚目的焦點；同理，**steal the limelight** 是「搶盡風頭」。Matthew Henson 北極之行回國後 was pushed out of the limelight 當然就是黯然成為醜小鴨，而不是跟 Robert Edwin Peary 一樣飛上枝頭成鳳凰，所以答案就是 (A)。

❷ 一個人重視 credit「信用」，就是 honest「可信的」，當然是一種 honor，因此 credit 會引申出「榮耀」的意思。反過來看，**honor** 當動詞用時也有「信守」之意，例如：to honor a promise「信守承諾」。 (C) (D) 選項的 credit 都應該做 honor 解，所以 take all the credit 是把功勞全部搶走之意。

從拆解歷史類題目，看看補述用法的角色

## ⚙️ 深度應用分析：對付閱讀就是要化「繁」為「簡」。先刪去( )、[ ] 內的文字，找出主要的主詞和動詞！

**❶** While (Peary and his crew returned home heroes and were showered with medals and adulation), (Henson was left unnoticed and unmentioned until more than 30 years later).

### 👉 解析

**❶** 這句話結構極為單純。唯一重點是後面的主要子句 Henson was left unnoticed and unmentioned…later。英文有一些不完全及物動詞後面接受詞和受詞補語，例如：wipe the floor clean（把地板擦乾淨）、pull a drawer open（把抽屜拉開）、push the door shut（把門關上）、leave the baby unattended（放任嬰兒無人照顧）等。

Henson was left unnoticed and unmentioned 只不過是將 leave 從主動改為被動。

**❷** (Henson's ability to communicate with the guides in their own language and his knowledge of navigation) made him indispensable.

### 解析

**❶** 這句話主詞很長，整個括弧框起來的都是主詞；made 也是不完全及物動詞，後面接受詞 him 以及受詞補語 indispensable

**❷** indispensable = in(not) + dis(away) + pens(hang) + able (形容詞字尾)

這字太長了，先從核心部分 dispense 談起

字根 pens、pend 意即 hang，從這意思會引申為秤子、天平，因為它們都是懸吊裝置。這字根衍生出一批有關買賣的字眼，像 spend、expense、pound。言歸正傳，服用藥必須定量，因此藥商必須仔細論斤秤兩後再 give away 給客人，**dispense** 字根結構就是這樣，所以是「分配、配藥」，名詞 **dispensary** 是「藥房」。可是有時少部分備用藥是隨主藥配送的，例如看感冒會附送退燒藥，看關節炎會附送止痛藥，假如沒有特殊狀況，這些藥可以省略不必服用。照這種情況解讀，**dispense with** 意即「免除、省去」。形容詞 **dispensable** 可以免除省去，所以是「可有可無的」。再加上否定字首 in-，**indispensable** 絕不能免除省去，所以是「不可或缺的」，

*eH* 1

*eH* 2

*eH* 3

*eH* 4

*eH* 5

從拆解歷史類題目，看看補述用法的角色

*eH* 6

# Peaks and Politics (1)

## 國家公園政治學（1）

💡 閱讀原文：試用 3 分鐘的時間念完文章，記得先把中文遮上，並翻頁看題目問什麼。計時開始！

### Peaks and Politics (1)

Rising straight up from the valley floor, the Teton Mountains **thrust** into the sky like huge **spears**. On some days, the snow-tipped peaks seem close enough to touch; on others, they appear aloof and unapproachable, **smothered** by clouds. Most people probably don't know that this small corner of the world was once the setting for political **upheaval**. It took more than fifty years to resolve the **strife** among conservationists, big-game hunters, dude ranchers, cattle barons, and politicians.

The first attempt to turn the Tetons into a national park took place in 1898, when the suggestion was made to **annex** it to nearby Yellowstone Park. Cattle ranch owners, fearing the loss of valuable grazing land, defeated the proposal. After World War I the price of beef plunged, and cattle breeders needed a new way to make a living: dude ranches that sounded like an American version of the African big game hunt and **lured** easterners to the romantic West, where they could play at being cowboys. Soon hot-dog stands, cheap motels, and souvenir shops **defiled** the beauty of the area.

## 國家公園政治學（**1**）

提頓山從河谷拔地而起，像根長矛插入天際。有些日子白雪覆蓋的山頂似乎近在眼前伸手可及；有些日子雲霧繚繞似乎遠在天邊只可遠觀。大部分人可能都不知道世上這麼一個小小角落曾經上演過政治角力，要花 50 幾年才能平息這場保育人士、大型獵物狩獵玩家、休閒農場、養牛大戶、政客之間的紛爭。

第一次打算把提頓山改成國家公園是發生在 1898 年，那時是提議把它併入附近的黃石公園。養牛大戶擔心失去寶貴的牧地，把這提案擋了下來。第一次世界大戰以後，牛肉價格直直落，養牛大戶亟需一種養家活口的新招數——休閒農場，乍聽之下彷彿是美國版的非洲大型獵物狩獵活動，吸引東部人來到浪漫的西部，在那裏他們可以假扮成牛仔。熱狗攤、便宜汽車旅館、紀念品商店很快就玷污了這地區的美。

**According to the passage, which is NOT true of the dude ranch?**
(A) It was a type of ranch oriented towards visitors.
(B) It invited wealthy people from the East Coast to experience the cowboy lifestyle.
(C) It originated from African and spread to America after World War I.
(D) It might result in uncontrolled commercial exploitation and spoil the Teton Mountains' magnificence.

根據本篇文章，以下哪一點對休閒農場的描述不是正確的？
(A) 它是一種以遊客為導向的農場
(B) 它邀請美國東岸的有錢大爺來體驗牛仔生活方式
(C) 它起源自非洲，第一次大戰以後傳進美國
(D) 它可能導致商業開發亂象，讓提頓山的雄偉蒙塵

👉 解析

答案 | (C)

❶ 這一題答案就藏在第二段倒數第二句 After World War I...play at being cowboys。從這句話可以知道 (A) (B) 陳述都正確，但是 (C) 錯誤，因為休閒農場跟非洲狩獵很像，但

是並不意味起源自非洲。根據下一句 Soon hot-dog stands…the area 也能知道 (D) 陳述正確。

❷ plunge 來自一個很沉重的單字家族，這家族的大家長是 plumb「鉛錘、垂直的」，鉛的化學元素符號 Pb 就是這個字。

其它的相關成員有：

plumber = plumb + er(名詞字尾)「水管工人」。鉛延展性極佳，既不容易腐蝕，也不容易破裂，所以打從羅馬帝國以來就一直拿來做水管，直到現代才發現會導致重金屬中毒，改用不鏽鋼管或塑膠管。

aplomb = a(to) + plomb。鉛的沉重特性引申到人的性格，當然是指一個人「沉著」，這種穩重的特質則是來自於「自信」。

鉛的沉重特性容易讓人聯想到掉落，所以 plummet 是「垂直落下」，此外還有 plunge「掉進、下跌」、plump「墜下、沉重地」、plop「落下、撲通聲」、plunk「放下、撲通聲」。

❶ After World War I the price of beef plunged, and cattle breeders needed a new way to make a living: dude ranches[that sounded like an American version of the African big game hunt and lured easterners to the romantic West, (where they could play at being cowboys)].

👉 解析

❶ 冒號後面的 dude ranches 是前面 a new way 的同位語，補充說明第一次大戰後養牛戶餬口的新方法是轉型成休閒農場。這種用法的同位語重述了前面主要子句所要傳達的訊息，而且有製造文章高潮的效果，尤其是同位語只是一個單字或片語時。冒號的作用不只表示暫停，而且還提醒讀者，後面還要揭露更重要的事情。例如：

Most contemporary philosophies echo ideas from one man: Plato, a student of Socrates and the teacher of Alexander.

（大部分當代哲學都附和一個人的思想：柏拉圖，也就是蘇格拉底的弟子和亞歷山大的老師。）

❷ that 是關係代名詞帶領子句修飾前面的先行詞 dude ranches。後面小括號框起來的是關係副詞 where 帶領的子句修飾前面的 the romantic West。

❷ On some days, the snow-tipped peaks seem close enough to touch; on others, they appear aloof and unapproachable, smothered by clouds.

👉 解析

❶ 這句話的 seem 和 appear 都是連綴動詞，後面接形容詞作主詞補語。

❷ 連綴動詞除了常見的 look、sound、smell、taste、feel、get、become、grow、turn、keep、stay、remain、seem、appear 等，還包含以下幾個：

His hypothesis **proves** incorrect.

（他的假設是不對的。）

The horse **fell** lame.

（那馬瘸了。）

go 之後通常跟貶義形容詞，表示向不好的方面發展。例如：

The beggar **went** blind at the age of twelve.

（這乞丐 12 歲時就失明了。）

# Peaks and Politics (2)

## 國家公園政治學（2）

💡 閱讀原文：試用 3 分鐘的時間念完文章，記得先把中文遮上，並翻頁看題目問什麼。計時開始！

### Peaks and Politics (2)

To rescue the Tetons, Horace Albright, **superintendent** of Yellowstone, **escorted** industrialist John D. Rockefeller Jr. on a trip through the mountains. (A) Since Rockefeller's very name would have increased land prices, Albright suggested that Rockefeller form a secret company to purchase land in the area. (B) When it was learned that Rockefeller had bought much of the valley to **deed** it to the nation for a national park, **tumult** resulted. The first Grand Teton National Park was established in 1929, but Rockefeller's gift of more than 33,000 acres was refused. (C) His act of pure altruism was interpreted as an invasive attempt to cheat poor **homesteaders**. (D)

In 1942, Rockefeller informed President Franklin D. Roosevelt that if the National Park Service would not take over the land, he was going to sell it. When Roosevelt accepted the gift by executive privilege, Congress passed a law to stop it, which the president, in turn, vetoed. Another eight years passed before all the land that Rockefeller had bought, plus the earlier national park, was turned into the Grand Teton National Park.

## 國家公園政治學（2）

為了搶救提頓山，黃石公園的園長何瑞斯·奧布萊陪同工業鉅子約翰洛克斐勒去那裡走一趟。因為單靠洛克斐勒的大名就能哄抬地價，奧布萊建議洛克斐勒成立一家地下公司蒐購該地區土地。(A) 當大家知道洛克斐勒把大部分山谷買下來，打算轉讓給國家成立國家公園時，引發了騷動。(B) 1929 年最早的大提頓國家公園成立了，但是卻把洛克斐勒那片超過 33000 英畝的大禮拒之門外。(C) 他這種無私的行為被解讀成對貧窮的自耕農巧取豪奪。(D)

1942 年，洛克斐勒告知羅斯福總統，假如國家公園管理局不接管那些土地，他就要賣掉。羅斯福以行政官員豁免權接受這份大禮時，國會卻通過一個法條加以阻止，總統再否決那個法條還以顏色。又過了八年，所有洛克斐勒蒐購的土地，加上先前的國家公園，整個變成大提頓國家公園。

Look at the four letters that indicate where the following sentence could be added to the passage.

**Actually, the vilification of Rockefeller came mostly from the cattlemen, who were afraid that the Park Service would not allow them free access to the valley grazing lands.**

Where could the sentence best fit?

看看文章裡四個字母，哪個地方可以把下面句子安插進去

**事實上，對洛克斐勒的中傷絕大部分都是那些養牛大戶下的毒手，因為他們害怕國家公園管理局會不准他們免費使用山谷裡的牧地。**

這句子放哪裡最合適？

 解析

答案｜(D)

❶ 題目這句話雖然沒有代名詞、指示詞，但是卻有關鍵名詞 vilification

❷ vilification = vil (vile) + ific (make) + ation (名詞字尾)「中傷」。這字落落長令人看了心慌慌，但是解析到最小單位可

238

以發現它就是 vile 的名詞。可能很多人都不認識 vile，但是它的表親 vend「出售、叫賣」就比較眼熟了。另一個表親 **venal**「貪污的」是形容一個人良心、道德，甚至靈魂都可以喊價格。字義朝著貶抑人格的方向發展，到了 **vile** 就變成「低廉的、卑劣的」。動詞 **vilify** 使人家評價變得很卑劣，所以是「毀謗」。vile 的同門兄弟 **vice**「惡行、邪惡」也遺傳到壞基因，形容詞 **vicious**「邪惡的、惡性的」。

❸ 從整句話加上前一篇文章所提到資訊，可以合理假設 Rockefeller 好心沒好報受到惡意誣衊，而發動這攻擊的幕後黑手可能又是對成立國家公園一貫持反對態度的養牛大戶，因為成立國家公園以後他們會受到法規的約束無法為所欲為。vilification 則是指 an invasive attempt to cheat poor homesteaders，所以答案是 (D)。

⚙ **深度應用分析：對付閱讀就是要化「繁」為「簡」。先刪去( )、[ ] 內的文字，找出主要的主詞和動詞！**

❶ Actually, the vilification of Rockefeller came mostly from the cattlemen, (who were afraid that the Park Service would not allow them free access to the valley grazing lands).

## 🔷 解析

❶ who 帶領關係子句括號裡面的修飾先行詞 the cattlemen，裡面的形容詞 afraid 是附屬子句的主詞補語

❷ 大家只知道關係代名詞、同位語有補述用法、限定用法，殊不知其實形容詞也有。形容詞補述用法主要跟連綴動詞有關；限定用法又分成前位修飾跟後位修飾。所謂前位修飾是形容詞放在所修飾的名詞前面；同理，後位修飾則是放在後面，例如：

A white elephant is rare.　　white 是前位修飾，rare 是後位修飾

❸ 英文凡是 a-為首的副詞做形容詞用時，通常只做補述用法，也就是說這些形容詞往往只出現在連綴動詞後面。這些形容詞有：afraid、alive、ablaze「閃爍的」、averse「反對的」、alone、alike、afloat、ashamed、alert「警覺的」、aloof「疏遠的」、asleep、awake、aghast「目瞪口呆的」、aglow「發光的」、adrift「漂流的」。例如：

I am averse to using chemicals in my garden.
（我不願意在自己花園施用農藥。）

❷ His act of pure altruism was interpreted as an invasive attempt to cheat poor homesteaders.

### 👉 解析

❶ 這句話結構簡單，後面的 an invasive attempt to cheat poor homesteaders 是主詞 His act of pure altruism 的補語

❷ 這句話是 People interpreted his act of pure altruism as an invasive attempt to cheat poor homesteaders 的被動版本。Interpret 意思是「將…解釋為…」，後面的 his act of pure altruism 是受詞，而 as 後面的 an invasive attempt to cheat poor homesteaders 則是受詞補語。相同用法的情況還有「將…看成…」，單字方面有 view、take、regard、see、deem、perceive，片語方面則有 think of、refer to、look upon，後面也都是接「受詞 + as + 受詞補語」。例如：

We viewed his scientific achievements as tremendous.

= His scientific achievement was viewed as tremendous (by us).

= his scientific achievement was thought of as tremendous.

（他科學上的成就被視為很了不起。）

# Meaningful Measurement (1)

## 放諸四海皆準（1）

💡 閱讀原文：試用 **3** 分鐘的時間念完文章，記得先把中文遮上，並翻頁看題目問什麼。計時開始！

**Meaningful Measurement (1)**

Such controversy - how many of one thing is worth how many of another? - has almost always been decided by the strongest or most powerful person in societies of every kind. So it is little surprise that many units of measure were based on the leader's body. One of the earliest examples of this, the **cubit**, the distance from the tip of the middle finger to the point of the elbow of an Egyptian pharaoh, was used in the construction of the pyramids. However, as pharaohs came and went, the system of measurement was thrown **askew**. Not all pharaohs were the same size; some were even small boys. A more familiar unit of measure, the foot, was based on the length of a British king's foot. This **chaotic** approach also brought us units of measurement such as the rod, the chain, the karat, and the **gill**. Since each unit of measurement was arrived at independently, the number of feet in, for example, a rod or a yard was determined by pure chance.

## 放諸四海皆準（1）

　　某東西多少個可以換另一種東西多少個──這種爭議幾乎總是由各種社會中塊頭最壯的、權力最大的說了算，因此以領導人的身體為依據訂出許多測量單位便不足為奇了。這種情況最早的案例之一就是建造金字塔時使用到的「腕尺」，也就是埃及法老王從中指指尖到手肘這段距離。然而隨著一任又一任的法老王，這套測量系統整個走樣了。不是所有法老王身材都一樣，有的甚至還是小男孩。英呎這種大家熟悉的測量單位就是以英國國王的腳為依據。這種混亂的方式下就出現了桿、測鏈、克拉、及耳這些測量單位。既然每個測量單位都是各自量出來的，那麼一桿、一碼到底有多少英呎就隨機決定了。

從拆解歷史類題目，看看補述用法的角色

**Which of the following best expresses the essential information in the underlined sentence? Incorrect answer choices change the meaning in important ways or leave out essential information.**

(A) Since there is no universal criterion for a fair deal, it is usually the most influential person who calls the shots.

(B) When there is a conflict over the price, it is often up to the person in charge to make sure to give everyone a fair shake.

(C) The person in control of group usually has the final say on whether to trade one thing for another or not.

(D) The most advantaged person always gets a reasonable price when he or she barters with other people.

以下哪一句最能表達出劃底線句子的基本訊息？不正確的答案選項會以重要方式改變句義，或者遺漏基本訊息

(A) 因為公平交易沒有通用準則，通常是影響力最大的人說了算。

(B) 價格上有爭議時，通常是由負責的人來確定是不是對每個人都一視同仁。

(C) 是否要以物易物總是由管理整個群體的人拍板定案。

(D) 最佔優勢的人跟別人以物易物時，總是價格最公道。

## 解析

答案 | **(A)**

❶ **(A)** 選項的 **call the shot** 這個說法源自於炮兵部隊。隨著火炮製造技術愈來愈精良，炮彈愈打愈遠，甚至打到比眼睛看得到還遠的地方，所以必須派出一個人跑到前線，當後方火炮的耳目，這個人叫作前進觀測官。前進觀測官觀察彈著點，以無線電指揮後方的火炮怎麼調整方向、修正仰角，這就叫 **call the shot**「發號施令、當家作主」。交易過程只要你情我願即可，本來就沒有一定的準則，最後往往取決於佔優勢的一方，正好跟題目句吻合，所以答案是 **(A)**。

❷ **(B)** 選項的 **a fair shake** 本來應該是 a fair shake of the dice，還有很多種變化，像 a fair crack of the whip、a fair suck of the sauce bottle，美國總統 Obama 甚至還常常說 a fair shot。再怎麼千變萬化，永遠都不變的是 fair「公平的」。賭博為了表示沒有耍老千，每個賭徒搖骰子時務必老老實實，搖多少下、怎麼搖都要一模一樣，這就是 a fair shake (of the dice)，意思是「一視同仁、機會均等」。

eH 1
eH 2
eH 3
eH 4
eH 5
從拆解歷史題目，看看補述用法的角色
eH 6

## ⚙ 深度應用分析：對付閱讀就是要化「繁」為「簡」。先刪去( )、[ ] 內的文字，找出主要的主詞和動詞！

**❶** Such controversy - how many of one thing is worth how many of another? - has almost always been decided by the strongest or most powerful person in societies of every kind.

### 👉 解析

**❶** How many of one thing is worth how many of another 是 Such controversy 的修飾語，插入句子中間補充説明自古以來交易過程物件換算出現紛爭最後往往是強者主導一切。這個修飾語也可以搬到 Such controversy 前面，自己獨立成一句。

**❷** 破折號表示強烈停頓，提醒讀者隨後即將出現重要訊息。像這樣的修飾語插入句子中間，破折號必定成雙成對出現。

**❸** 整句所要表達的思想可以被修飾語暫時打斷，這個修飾語可以是單字、片語、句子都行。假如修飾語句子是直述句，修飾語句尾不須打逗點；假如是問句、驚嘆句，修飾語句尾還是要加上原本應有的問號、驚嘆號。例如：

An important question about education — should universities teach the classics or just courses in science and practical subjects? — was the topic of a famous debate by Chohan and Coppin.

（大學應該教經典名著，還是只開科學與實用學科的課程？這個關於教育的重要問題是 Chohan 和 Coppin 一場有名辯論的題目。）

❷ One of the earliest examples of this, (the cubit, the distance from the tip of the middle finger to the point of the elbow of an Egyptian pharaoh), was used in the construction of the pyramids.

## 👉 解析

❶ TOEFL 的文章很像學術論文，難免會出現一些專業術語。為了避免考題對某一種專業的考生特別有利，一定會針對這些術語做解釋，尤其是利用同位語。

❷ the cubit 是 One of the earliest examples of this 的同位語。由於 cubit 這個字太冷僻，所以後面再出現另一個同位語 the distance from the tip of the middle finger to the point of the elbow of an Egyptian pharaoh 告訴讀者 cubit 到底是什麼意思。

# Meaningful Measurement (2)

## 放諸四海皆準（2）

### Meaningful Measurement (2)

In the last decade of the eighteenth century, the French Revolution resulted in the **dissolution** of the monarchy. Some scientists realized that, because everything else was changing, they had a unique opportunity to **impose** order on the **archaic** system of measurement, which they deplored, and to establish a more appropriate and more coherent system for modern science and society. (A) They knew that the **crux** of their problem was the variance in units of measure, so they decided to **predicate** the new units of measure on nature. (B) For the basis of their system, they chose a tiny fraction of the distance from the **equator** to the North Pole. They named this unit the meter. (C) For ease of computation, they divided the meter into ten subdivisions called decimeters. Decimeters were divided into centimeters, and centimeters into millimeters. Namely, all conversions within this system are in base 10. (D)

## 放諸四海皆準（2）

在 18 世紀最後十年，法國大革命導致君主政體瓦解。因為一切都在改變，有些科學家意識到他們當前有個很難得的機會，可以給為人詬病的老掉牙測量系統來個撥亂反正，為現代科學與社會建立起一套更合適、更一致的系統。(A) 他們知道問題的關鍵就在於測量單位的混亂，所以決定根據自然界來制定新的測量單位。(B) 他們選擇從赤道到北極這段距離的一小部分作為這套系統的基礎，將這單位稱呼為公尺。(C) 為了方便計算，再把公尺細分成十個分米，分米再分成公分，公分再分成公厘。也就是說，這系統內所有換算都是以十為基準。(D)

Look at the four letters that indicate where the following sentence could be added to the passage.

**Thus was born what we now call the metric system, which, an internationally agreed decimal system of measurement, is used internationally and almost exclusively in scientific fields.**

Where could the sentence best fit?

看看文章裡四個字母，哪個地方可以把下面句子安插進去

我們現在稱呼為「公制」的這套系統於焉誕生，這是國際公認的十進位測量體制，國際通用而且在科學界裡更是僅此一家別無分號。

這句子放哪裡最合適？

## 解析

答案 | **(D)**

❶ 題目這句話有個關鍵名詞 the metric system，而且根據本句描述，都已經是 internationally agreed。一套制度要 is used internationally and almost exclusively in scientific fields，肯定要假以時日，不可能一推出，馬上被大家接受

❷ (A) (B) (C) 選項基本上都還卡在這套測量制度是如何制訂出來的過程，因此很快就知道答案就是 (D)。

❸ 形容詞的補述用法有一個句型很重要——「it be 形容詞+ 介系詞+ 名詞+ 不定詞」。it 是虛主詞，真正主詞是後面的不定詞片語，形容詞是主詞補語。

例如：

It is easy for her to get angry.

（她很容易發火。）

It is polite of him to hold the door for the old man.

（他為老人頂住門，很有禮貌。）

❹ metric 是 meter 的形容詞。meter 和 measure 關係十分密切，因為 meter「公尺」是一種 measure「測量」單位，而且只要各自去掉名詞字尾，字根部分其實是一樣的：meter = met + er(名詞字尾)；measure = meas + ure(名詞字尾)。凡是出現 meter 字根的單字大多要解讀成 measure，例如：

diameter = dia(across) + meter「直徑」。

perimeter = peri(around) + meter「圓周」。

thermometer = thermos(temperature) + meter「溫度計」。

symmetry = sym(same) + metr(meter) + y(名詞字尾)。

「對稱」是每個部位測量數據都一樣。

❶ Thus was born what we now call the metric system, [which,(an internationally agreed decimal system of measurement),is used internationally and almost exclusively in scientific fields].

## 👉 解析

❶ 這是一個倒裝句。主詞是 what we now call the metric system，不只後面出現小括弧框起來的同位語，還出現中括弧框起來的補述用法關係子句要修飾它。尾隨的跟班一大堆，主詞顯得很長，所以倒裝放句尾，才不至於讓整個句子頭重腳輕。

❷ 打上逗號的關係子句叫補述用法，跟限定用法不同，例如：
The dog which the car ran over belonged to our neighbor. （被車子輾到的那隻狗是我們鄰居養的。）這句是限定用法。關係代名詞可以改用 that，也可以省略。關係子句 which the car ran over 是必要資訊，一旦刪掉，讀者會不知道哪一隻狗。

The dog, which the car ran over, belonged to our

neighbor.（那隻狗是我們鄰居養的，被車子輾到了。）這句是補述用法。關係代名詞不能改用 that，也不能省略。關係子句 which the car ran over 是順便一提的資訊，讀者已經知道是哪隻狗，即使刪掉關係子句，也不妨礙讀者的認知。

❷ Some scientists realized {that, because everything else was changing, they had a unique opportunity [to impose order on the archaic system of measurement, (which they deplored)], and [to establish a more appropriate and more coherent system for modern science and society]}.

## 👉 解析

❶ 小括弧裡的 which 關係子句修飾 the archaic system of measurement，形容原有那一套測量制度大家用得叫苦連天。

❷ 中括弧裡的兩個不定詞片語是要修飾 a unique opportunity，說明這個天賜良機可以讓他們做兩件事，一個是除舊，一個是布新。

❸ 大括弧裡的 that 子句做 realized 的受詞，也就是科學家們發現因為當時一切都天翻地覆，而這種亂局正好也提供一個送往迎來的契機。

# The Rocket's Red Glare (1)

# 火箭的紅烈焰（1）

 閱讀原文：試用 3 分鐘的時間念完文章，記得先把中文遮上，並翻頁看題目問什麼。計時開始！

### The Rocket's Red Glare (1)

In the 17th century, Sir Isaac Newton published his Third Law: For every action there is an equal and opposite reaction. This simple rule of nature is the basis for the rockets that **catapult** both bombs and people into the air. The first mention of rockets appeared in various Chinese writings of the 13th century, in which several writers reported rockets being used and expected to have driven off Mongol invaders. Why rockets were invented in China is anyone's guess. Some historians **surmise** that the high levels of **sulfur** and **potassium nitrate** in the soil may have been accidentally kicked into a campfire, resulting in an explosion. The transition from explosion to rocketry required an additional step. When this explosion is created in a hollow tube that is capped on one end, the force of the explosion is **vented** through a single opening. This "action" in one direction moves the tube in an "equal and opposite" direction. The force of the discharge can be increased or decreased by widening or narrowing the opening.

## 火箭的紅烈焰（1）

17 世紀時，牛頓發表了運動第三定律：每個作用力都有一股反作用力，大小相等、方向相反。可以把炸彈和人投射到空中的火箭就是根據這條簡單的自然規則。13 世紀中國人諸多著作中都提到火箭首次出現，作者描述使用火箭，寄望這玩意可以把蒙古入侵者拒之門外。沒有人知道何以中國會發明火箭。有些歷史學家猜測可能是不小心把硫與硝酸鉀含量很高的土壤踢進營火裡導致爆炸。可是從爆炸到火箭還需要額外的臨門一腳。將空管一端塞住，裡面產生爆炸時，爆炸的力量會從唯一的開口排放出來。朝著某個方向的作用力會以相等的力道讓這管子朝著相反方向移動。透過開口孔徑的縮放可以控制所釋放的力道大小。

**According to this passage, which is NOT true of rockets?**

(A) Rockets are based on Newton's Third Law.

(B) By the 13th century the Chinese had developed the first rockets and used them to repel the invasion of Mongol successfully.

(C) The first step in the development of rocketry was the discovery that some materials can cause an explosion when they are ignited.

(D) A rocket can channel explosive force to create thrust.

根據這篇文章，對火箭的陳述哪一個是不正確的？

(A) 火箭所根據的原理是牛頓第三運動定律。

(B) 到了 13 世紀中國人已經開發出第一款火箭並且用這東西成功的擊退蒙古的入侵。

(C) 火箭發展的第一步是發現某些物質引燃時會引發爆炸。

(D) 火箭可以引導爆炸力的排放方向，從而產生推力。

解析

答案｜(B)

❶ 從第一段第二句可以知道 (A) 選項陳述正確。

❷ 整段中間 Some historians surmise that…resulting in an explosion 這句話可以證實 (C) 選項陳述正確。

❸ 從 The transition from explosion to rocketry required an additional step 這句話以下都是在解釋怎麼引導爆炸力，使之產生反作用力，所以 (D) 選項陳述正確。

❹ 第一段第三句 The first mention of rockets…expected to have driven off Mongol invaders 最關鍵的就是 expected to have driven off Mongol invaders，不定詞完成式意味使用火箭逐退蒙古人的這個期待最後夢碎，因此 (B) 選項陳述錯誤。

❺ **invade** 的字根 vade 意即 go，不難理解其字義「入侵」。其他同源字還有

**evade** = e(out) + vade(go)。字根結構 go out 看起來是奪門而出，走為上策，所以是「逃避」。形容詞 evasive 把「溜」之大吉的涵義表現得更加淋漓盡致「難以捉住的」。

**pervade** = per(through) + vade(go)。介系詞 through 有從頭到尾整個的意思，所以是「遍及、瀰漫」。

**extravagant** = extra(out) + vag(go) + ant(形容詞字尾)。字首 e-、ex-、extra- 意思都是 out。字根結構一看就有逾越的感覺，所以是「越軌的、放肆的、浪費的」。

*eH* 1

*eH* 2

*eH* 3

*eH* 4

*eH* 5

*eH* 6

從拆解科學、科技類題目，看不定詞、動名詞的角色

## 深度應用分析：對付閱讀就是要化「繁」為「簡」。先刪去( )、[ ] 內的文字，找出主要的主詞和動詞！

**❶** The first mention of rockets appeared in various Chinese writings of the 13th century, [in which several writers reported rockets (being used and expected to have driven off Mongol invaders)].

### ☞ 解析

**❶** 中括弧框起來的關係子句修飾 various Chinese writings of the 13th century，說明好幾位作家都在古籍裡提過火箭的使用。

**❷** 小括弧框起來的動名詞片語是要修飾 rockets，其中不定詞寫成完成式 to have p.p.的形式意味當初第一次在戰場上施放火箭，原先期待這種新武器可以把蒙古入侵者趕走，可是事實上事與願違。

**❸** 不只是 expect，像 hope、wish、intend、mean、desire 之類的動詞都可以套用這種不定詞完成式，而且都是暗示最後想法落空，例如：James hoped to have won the lottery. = James hoped to win the lottery but he did not.

（James 希望可以中樂透，但是槓龜了。）

注意假如後面接一般不定詞，而非不定詞完成式，結果如何就未可知了，例如：

James hoped to win the lottery.

= James hoped that he would win the lottery.

（James 希望可以中樂透，結果如何尚無下文。）

**❷** When this explosion is created in a hollow tube (that is capped on one end), the force of the explosion is vented through a single opening.

### 解析

**❶** 括弧框起來的關係子句 that is capped on one end 修飾 a hollow tube。

**❷** cap 是「帽子、蓋子」，這一句當動詞用意思是「給…加上蓋子、堵住」。雖然看起來不甚起眼，其實 cap 是一個英文字根家族的大家長，這個家族的共同基因是 head。這家族瓜瓞綿綿，可說族繁不及備載，限於篇幅只能略舉下例：

cape「海角」是向海洋延伸出去的陸地，宛如探頭出來；海角另一個稱呼 headland 也是這個道理。

259

# The Rocket's Red Glare (2)

## 火箭的紅烈焰（2）

💡 閱讀原文：試用 **3** 分鐘的時間念完文章，記得先把中文遮上，並翻頁看題目問什麼。計時開始！

### The Rocket's Red Glare (2)

As with the 13th century Chinese, the first application of this technology in Europe was in weaponry. The ability to send balls of fire at a distant enemy offered a clear advantage in battle, but it's a pity there was no making them more accurate The problem was accuracy. On land, the cannon provided greater leverage for an army because its aim was more precise and its performance more reliable. On the other hand, the equipment required for launching rockets proved too **cumbersome** to move and set up under fire or in bad weather. However, it was at sea that the rocket proved itself to be a practical and effective weapon. The huge **canvas** sails and **tarred hull** of an enemy ship offered a perfect target. A single rocket could

**engulf** a ship in flames in a matter of minutes. As the accuracy of rockets increased, they began to play a part in ground warfare. The V-1 and V-2 rockets developed by the Germans in World War II terrified London. Today's intercontinental missiles with their atomic warheads are some of the most feared weapons in history.

## 火箭的紅烈焰（2）

　　就跟 13 世紀中國人一樣，在歐洲這種技術第一次應用是在武器上。戰場上要是可以朝遠方敵人猛砸火球當然佔盡便宜，但是很可惜沒辦法使之很精準。陸地上，大炮因為瞄得比較準，表現比較可靠，可以給軍隊帶來加分效果。但是另一方面，由於發射火箭所需要的裝置太過笨重以至於在戰火下或惡劣天氣下難以搬動架設。然而在海上，火箭就成為一種很實用、很有效的武器了。敵船上巨大的帆布和塗抹焦油的船殼都是很好瞄準的目標。一個火箭只需要幾分鐘就可以讓一艘船被熊熊大火吞噬。隨著精準度提升，火箭開始在地面戰爭佔有一席之地。二次世界大戰中，德國人所研製的 V1、V2 火箭震懾了整個倫敦。今天的原子彈頭洲際飛彈也是史上最令人膽顫心驚的武器。

**Which of the following best expresses the essential information in the underlined sentence? Incorrect answer choices change the meaning in important ways or leave out essential information.**

(A) There was evidence that the equipment required for launching rockets was difficult to carry, so rockets were never used under attack or on rainy days.

(B) The equipment necessary for launching rockets was so heavy and bulky that rockets turned out to be impractical on land.

(C) Rockets were put to proof in battle or in rainy days and found useless because the tools for launching rockets were very massive.

(D) The instruments for launching rockets were all too enormous to move from place to place easily at war or in bad weather.

以下哪一句最能表達出劃底線句子的基本訊息？不正確的答案選項會以重要方式改變句義，或者遺漏基本訊息

(A) 有證據顯示發射火箭的裝置難以攜帶，所以受到攻擊時或雨天從不使用火箭。

(B) 火箭的發射裝置非常笨重，以至於火箭在陸地上並不管用。

(C) 將火箭拿到戰場或雨天時測試，結果竟然因為發射裝置太過巨大，所以毫無用武之地。

(D) 火箭發射裝置非常巨大，在戰場上或惡劣天氣下很容易搬來搬去。

### 👉 解析

答案｜(B)

❶ 題目這句話的 prove 後面接主詞補語而非受詞，代表它是連綴動詞，意思也跟「證明」無關，例如：

Language barrier may prove insurmountable for some people.（對某些人而言，語言障礙可能難以克服。）

因此 (A) (C) 兩個選項都不對。

❷ (D) 選項語意有矛盾。too 前面出現 all、only、just、but 時，會等於 very，亦即 too…to… 這句型會失去的否定涵義，例如：

He is only too pleased to come to her assistance.

（我們非常喜歡看這部電視劇。）

We are but too glad to help you.

（我們非常樂意幫助你。）

(D) 選項這樣的敘述當然很離譜。綜上所言，答案非 (B) 莫屬

## ⚙️ 深度應用分析：對付閱讀就是要化「繁」為「簡」。先刪去( )、[ ] 內的文字，找出主要的主詞和動詞！

**❶** On the other hand, the equipment (required for launching rockets) proved too cumbersome to move and set up under fire or in bad weather.

### 👉 解析

**❶** 括弧框起來的分詞片語 required for launching rockets 是要修飾主詞 the equipment

**❷** prove 後面是表示最後結果的主詞補語，這種場合 prove 等於 turn out、come out、end up、end up，字義反而跟常見的「證明」無關

**❸** 注意不定詞句型 too…to…有否定的涵義，所以這裡是說火箭剛在歐洲戰場出現時，因為發射裝置太過笨重，導致在戰火或惡劣天氣下不方便移動、架設。注意這個句型有例外狀況，也就是假如結構中的形容詞是 apt、anxious、ready、easy、eager、willing 這些字眼時，會意味肯定，反而沒有否定的涵義，例如：

He is too ready to accept this constructive idea.

（他很樂意接受這個建設性的想法。）

He was too eager to know the result of the exams.

（他急於知道考試成績。）

此外也要注意寫成 can't…too…或 never too…時，意思是

「再……也不算太……」，例如：

It was wrong to think that one can't bear too many children.

（孩子再怎麼生也不算多，這種想法是錯的。）

An official can never be too careful in speaking in public.

（官員公開講話時愈小心愈好。）

❷ [The ability (to send balls of fire at a distant enemy) offered a clear advantage in battle], but [it's a pity (there was no making them more accurate)].

### 👉 解析

❶ 連接詞 but 連接兩個子句。不定詞片語 to send balls of fire at a distant enemy 修飾主要子句的主詞 The ability。後面附屬子句中 it's a pity 的 it 是虛主詞，真正的主詞是 there was no making them more accurate，前面有連接詞 that 被省略掉。代名詞 them 當然是指前面提到的 balls of fire。it is a pity 意即「很可惜」，What a pity! = What a shame!「真可惜」

❷ there is no 動名詞 = it is impossible 不定詞，意思是「沒辦法」或「不可以」。一般看到的標語 No littering「不准亂丟垃圾」，其實就是 There is no littering 的精簡版，這種場合就等於 You must not…。例如：

No talking in class. = There is no talking in class.= You must not talk in class.（上課不准講話。）

## Unit 6-3

# Autopsy: Examining the Dead to Understand the Living (1)

# 驗屍：未知死，焉知生（1）

💡 閱讀原文：試用 3 分鐘的時間念完文章，記得先把中文遮上，並翻頁看題目問什麼。計時開始！

### Autopsy: Examining the Dead
### to Understand the Living (1)

Regardless of one's beliefs about the spiritual life of the soul, the treatment of our earthly remains is a matter of considerable importance. In nearly all cultures, the desecration of a dead body, even the body of an enemy, is **abhorrent**, so extreme measures are taken to recover the victims of mining disasters, plane crashes, and other accidents in order that their bodies may be properly buried. The **cremated** remains of loved ones are usually handled with great **reverence**. They have been lovingly scattered over the sea, housed in **shrines**, and even shot into space.

It is little surprise then that the idea of cutting apart and studying a dead body is charged with deep emotions. The thought of cutting into the human body is said to have been deeply repugnant to the early Chinese and Muslims. In the Middle Ages, many Western civilizations **prohibited** such human dissection. Even today, authorizing an autopsy on the body of a loved one can be a **heart-wrenching** decision.

## 驗屍：未知死，焉知生（1）

　　無論一個人對靈魂的精神生命抱持什麼信仰，世俗遺體的處置都是相當重要的問題。幾乎所有文化中，褻瀆遺體，哪怕是敵人遺體，都令人不齒，因此會盡一切手段找回礦災、空難、其他重大意外的罹難者，好讓他們的遺體可以妥善埋葬。所愛的人遺體火化後通常都受到高規格的禮遇，依依不捨地撒向大海，恭奉在神龕，甚至射向太空。

　　把遺體切開研究這種觀念會一石激起千層浪就不足為奇。據說以前中國人和回教徒都極端排斥將人體開膛剖腹這種想法。中古世紀時，許多西方文明都禁止這種人體解剖。即使是今天，授權讓自己心愛的人接受驗屍，下決定時都可能撕心裂肺一樣難受。

*et* 1

*et* 2

*et* 3

*et* 4

*et* 5

*et* 6

從拆解科學、科技類題目，看不定詞、動名詞的角色

**Which of the following best expresses the essential information in the underlined sentence? Incorrect answer choices change the meaning in important ways or leave out essential information**

(A) It is said that in old times Chinese and Muslims considered it disgusting to perform autopsies.

(B) People said that the dissection of corpses was unacceptableto Chinese and Muslims.

(C) Word has it that an autopsy is highly offensive to Chinese and Muslims.

(D) The early Chinese and Muslims were said to oppose the idea of performing autopsies.

以下哪一句最能表達出劃底線句子的基本訊息？不正確的答案選項會以重要方式改變句義，或者遺漏基本訊息

(A) （現在）聽說古代中國人和回教徒都認為驗屍很噁心。

(B) （以前曾經）聽說中國人和回教徒（以前）難以接受大體解剖。

(C) （現在）謠傳中國人和回教徒（現在）都極端嫌惡驗屍這種事。

(D) （以前曾經）聽說早期中國人和回教徒都反對驗屍這種觀念。

## 解析

答案 | (A)

❶ 因為不定詞寫成完成式是特意要讀者注意到時間先後順序，所以這一題必須特別注意時間。從題目句的…is said to have been…可以知道，作者現在聽說驗屍這種想法以往讓古代中國人和回教徒很厭惡，這樣的時間邏輯只有 (A) 選項呈現出來。就算不知道不定詞完成式，但是從 early 這個字也能看得出來是以往很難接受，而不是現在。

❷ 看到 repugnant 一副魁梧的模樣，千萬別投降，把這個拆解開來是這個樣子 re(back) + pugn(fight) +ant(形容詞字尾) 原來字根 pugn 意思竟然是 fight「打鬥」！其他家族成員像 punch「重擊」、pounce「猛撲」個個摩拳擦掌、張牙舞爪，每個都不好惹。

pugnacious = pugnac + ious(形容詞字尾)「好鬥的」。

pugilist= pugil + ist(人)「拳擊師」。

impugn= im(in) + pugn「抨擊」。

repugn 可以解讀為還以重拳，所以是「反對、反抗」；形容詞 repugnant 會引發別人反感，所以是「討厭的」。

## ⚙️ 深度應用分析：對付閱讀就是要化「繁」為「簡」。先刪去( )、[ ] 內的文字，找出主要的主詞和動詞！

❶ The thought of cutting into the human body is said to have been deeply repugnant to the early Chinese and Muslims.

### 👉 解析

❶ 中文沒有時式，可是英文這種句子偏偏對時間概念非常敏感，所以作答時務必注意動作發生先後順序。把不定詞寫成完成式，也就是 to have p.p 這個樣子，代表這個動作發生在主要動詞發生的時間以前，例如：

I am sorry to have kept you waiting long.

（很抱歉讓你久等了。）

所以這句話意味，（現在）聽説早期中國人和回教徒（以前）對解剖大體的觀念是很排斥的。

❷ 此外，不定詞也可以寫成進行式，也就是 to be Ving，代表這個動作和主要動詞同時發生，例如：

I pretended to be sleeping.

（我假裝正在睡覺。）

She was found to be stealing money in the convenience store. （她在便利商店裡面偷東西時被人發現。）

❷ [In nearly all cultures, the desecration of a dead body, even the body of an enemy, is abhorrent], so [extreme measures are taken to recover the victims of mining disasters, plane crashes, and other accidents (in order that their bodies may be properly buried)].

### 🖝 解析

❶ 連接詞 so 連接兩個子句。小括弧框起來的 in order that their bodies may be properly buried 是表示目的的介系詞片語

❷ 主要子句 the desecration of a dead body is abhorrent 結構簡單，主詞是 the desecration of a dead body，隨後插入 even the body of an enemy 補充說明侵犯大體極度令人極度排斥，即使是敵人也不例外。

❸ 比較複雜的是 so 後面的附屬子句，這是一個被動結構，但是 extreme measures are taken 後面的不定詞片語 to recover the victims of mining disasters, plane crashes, and other accidents 是要修飾前面的主詞 extreme measures，說明這些極端手段就是要找回各種天災人禍罹難者遺體。

# Autopsy: Examining the Dead to Understand the Living (2)

## 驗屍：未知死，焉知生（2）

🔅 閱讀原文：試用 3 分鐘的時間念完文章，記得先把中文遮上，並翻頁看題目問什麼。計時開始！

**Autopsy: Examining the Dead
to Understand the Living (2)**

It was not until the Renaissance that the dissection and study of **corpses** became an acceptable scientific practice. Many autopsies were performed in Renaissance Italy, and the Church did not object. (A) Only then was it possible to differentiate between the normal and abnormal appearances of human organs and to begin to link certain **symptoms** of a disease with observable abnormalities. Until the nineteenth century, autopsies were limited to observations that could be made with the naked eye. (B) Modern scientifically **sophisticated** autopsies require comprehensive chemical analysis.

(C) In addition to their scientific applications, modern autopsies have important legal significance. An autopsy can often determine whether death was the result of foul play or natural causes. The **pathologist** in such cases must be thorough and objective, listing all **lethal** and nonlethal facts uncovered during the examination of the body. (D) Determining the cause of death requires a broad-based examination of the body, the scene of the death, and all related circumstances.

## 驗屍：未知死，焉知生（2）

要一直到文藝復興，遺體的解剖與研究才總算成為大家認同的科學實習。當時義大利就進行過幾次驗屍，羅馬教會也沒反對。(A) 只有在那時候才有辦法區分人類器官外表正常與不正常的差異，開始將某個疾病的症狀跟所觀察到的畸形連結起來。直到 19 世紀，驗屍都還只侷限於肉眼所能做的觀察而已。(B) 現代科學精密驗屍還需要進行廣泛的化學分析。

(C) 除了科學應用外，現代驗屍在法律上也意義非凡。驗屍通常可以判斷死亡到底是肇因於他殺或自然因素。病理學家在這種情況下必須要仔細客觀，把驗屍時所發現的致命與非致命因素通通羅列出來。(D) 判斷死因必須針對屍體、死亡現場、所有相關環境進行廣泛的檢驗。

 **考題演練及解析**

Look at the four letters that indicate where the following sentence could be added to the passage.

**The microscope made it possible to study the changes in the cells and link their mutations with disease and death.**

Where could the sentence best fit?

看看文章裡四個字母，哪個地方可以把下面句子安插進去

顯微鏡問世以後才有辦法研究細胞的變化，將病變與疾病、死亡連結起來。

這句子放哪裡最合適？

👉 **解析**

答案 | (B)

❶ 題目句雖然有代名詞 it，但是它是虛受詞，跟前後句子無關，所以不能算是線索。儘管如此，microscope 卻是很難得的資訊，因為顯微鏡是近代科學萌芽時的產物，所以出現的時間不會太早。本文 (A) 選項前後文陳述都還停留在文藝復興時代，所以肯定不是答案。

❷ (B) 選項前面那句話一開頭就是 Until the nineteenth century⋯19 世紀顯微鏡早已問世了，不錯，這是一個好兆頭。句尾又提到⋯the naked eye 正好又和顯微鏡呼應，因此可以篤定答案應該就是 (B)。

❸ 假如題目句可以放進 (C) 選項，那麼它一定是主題句。看看題目句是有主題句的架勢，可是這樣還不夠，還得再檢視一下這一段隨後的句子有沒有一呼百諾的現象。也就是說，看看隨後句子有沒有圍繞著顯微鏡這個主題繼續闡述說明。很可惜，最末段放鴿子了，有關顯微鏡隻字片語都沒有。所以 (C) (D) 選項都錯誤。

e𝓭𝓽 1

e𝓭𝓽 2

e𝓭𝓽 3

e𝓭𝓽 4

e𝓭𝓽 5

e𝓭𝓽 6

從拆解科學、科技類題目，看不定詞、動名詞的角色

## ⚙ 深度應用分析：對付閱讀就是要化「繁」為「簡」。先刪去( )、[ ] 內的文字，找出主要的主詞和動詞！

**①** The microscope made it possible [to (study the changes in the cells) and (link their mutations with disease and death)].

### 👉 解析

**①** it 是虛受詞，真正的受詞是後面用中括弧框起來的不定詞片語，也就是說顯微鏡的問世讓兩件事成為可能，一件是研究細胞中的變化，一件是將這轉變跟疾病死亡搭起連結。最常套用這種句型的動詞還有 think、believe、find、consider、feel、believe、regard，例如：

The Internet makes it easier for companies to keep in touch with customers.

（網路讓公司跟客戶更容易保持聯繫。）

這種虛受詞句型也有一些慣用語，例如：

He makes it a practice/rule/habit to jog in the morning.

（他養成晨跑的習慣。）

People take it for granted to speak Chinese in China.

（大家都認為在中國說中文理所當然。）

❷ Only then was it possible [(to differentiate between the normal and abnormal appearances of human organs) and (to begin to link certain symptoms of a disease with observable abnormalities)].

## 👉 解析

❶ it 是虛主詞，真正的主詞是後面用中括弧框起來的不定詞片語

❷ only 後面接副詞、副詞片語、副詞子句放句首時，必須倒裝。例如：

Only slowly did she understand it.

（只有慢慢來她才能懂。）

Only with her can he find true love.

（只有與她共處時，他才能找到真愛。）

Only when one loses freedom does one know its value.

（唯有當一個人失去自由之後，他才知道自由的價值。）

💡 閱讀原文：試用 3 分鐘的時間念完文章，記得先
把中文遮上，並翻頁看題目問什麼。計時開始！

### An Uncommon Common Liquid (1)

Water, the most plentiful and commonplace of all liquids, is a **deceptively** simple **compound**. Each **molecule** of water consists of two atoms of hydrogen and one atom of oxygen. Scientific studies have ascertained that the hydrogen atoms are positioned on roughly the same side of the oxygen atom. This **configuration** gives water a very interesting property. Because the positive hydrogen atoms are on one side of the molecule and the negative oxygen atom is on the other, water molecules tend to adhere to one another. You can see evidence of this tendency if you place a drop of water on a smooth, flat surface. If you look closely you will see that it does not spread out. Instead it appears as a slightly flattened

**mound** held together by a tight "skin," which, sometimes called surface tension, also exists on large bodies of water, such as lakes and ponds. The surface of a pond is easy to walk across for an insect because the tension on the surface of the water is strong enough to support it.

## 水的平凡與不平凡（1）

　　所有液體中最豐富、最普通的是水，這種化合物看似簡單，但是不要被騙了。每一個水分子都由兩個氫原子和一個氧原子組成。科學研究早已確定氫原子位置約略跟氧原子同一側。這種結構讓水出現一種很有趣的屬性。因為帶正電的氫原子在分子的一側，帶負電的氧原子在另一側，水分子往往會互相依附。假如把水滴在平坦光滑的表面，你就能目睹水這種傾向的證據了。仔細觀察，就能看到水其實沒有擴散開來。相反的，它彷彿是一個稍微壓平的小土墩，外圍由一層「皮」緊緊包覆起來。這一層皮有時候叫做表面張力，也會出現在像是湖、池塘之類的大片水域。昆蟲可以輕鬆的在池塘表面凌波微步，就是因為水的表面張力大到可以撐住它。

 考題演練及解析

## This passage answers which of the following questions?

(A) What kind of small insect can walk on water?

(B) Why doesn't a metal boat sink?

(C) What makes a paper clip float?

(D) How does oxygen get into water?

以下哪一個問題可以在本篇文章找到解答？

(A) 哪一種小昆蟲可以在水面走路？

(B) 為什麼金屬船不會沉沒？

(C) 什麼因素讓迴紋針可以飄浮起來？

(D) 氧氣是怎樣溶入水中？

### 解析

答案｜(C)

❶ 綜觀本文很快就能找到重點：水的表面張力。只要把握這一點，這一題就能高枕無憂。

❷ 雖然文章後面提到因為水的表面張力這個特性，部分昆蟲才不至於慘遭沒頂，但是不能選 (A)，因為 (A) 顯然扯太遠了，已經超出化學領域，涉及生物、物理、數學多種層面。

❸ (B) 選項則是關於浮力，浮力跟表面張力是兩碼子的事，所以 (B) 也不對。

❹ (C) 選項的 paper clip 即「迴紋針」，迴紋針可以漂浮起來的道理跟小昆蟲並無二致，Bingo！答案非 (C) 莫屬。

❺ (D) 選項完全跟表面張力不相干，因此也不對。

❻ insect 跟 saw「鋸子」、sickle「鐮刀」是一家人

　insect = in(in) + sect(cut)

昆蟲是節肢動物，最明顯的特徵是身體可以分為頭、胸、腹，所以字根結構就是切成一截一截；

section = sect(cut) + tion (名詞字尾)「切片、段」。加上表示 in 的字首 inter-成為 intersection，要從「交流道」才能 cut in 高速公路；

dissect = dis(apart) + sect(cut)「解剖」。

sector = sect(cut) + or(名詞字尾)。圓切開的部分就是「扇形」。

Ch 1

Ch 2

Ch 3

Ch 4

Ch 5

Ch 6

從拆解科學、科技類題目，看不定詞、動名詞的角色

## 深度應用分析：對付閱讀就是要化「繁」為「簡」。先刪去( )、[ ] 內的文字，找出主要的主詞和動詞！

❶ (The surface of a pond is easy to walk across for an insect) because (the tension on the surface of the water is strong enough to support it).

### 解析

❶ because 連接兩個子句，兩句都有不定詞。前面這子句的 for an insect 特地搬到句尾，強調昆蟲可以藉由表面張力這個特性施展輕功踏雪無痕。換句話説，這句子原本應該是這樣

The surface of a pond is easy for an insect to walk across.

值得注意的是不及物動詞 walk 並不是沒有受詞，而是它的受詞正是前面的主詞 The surface of a pond，因此務必記住後面還要來個介系詞 across。總之，假如不定詞的動詞是不及物動詞時，一定要考慮該不該加上介系詞，例如：

The river is very dangerous to swim in.（在那條河裡游泳很危險。）主詞 The river 也是 swim 的受詞。

❷ 這種不定詞用法千萬不要跟表目的的不定詞 (in order) to 搞混，例如：

• I need a computer to work with.

（我工作需要一部電腦。）a computer 是不定詞 to work 的受詞，所以一定要保留介系詞 with

- I need a computer to work.

（為了工作，我需要一部電腦。）a computer 不是不定詞 to work 的受詞，所以沒必要加介系詞 with。

❷ Instead it appears as a slightly flattened mound held together by a tight "skin,"[which, (sometimes called surface tension), also exists on large bodies of water, such as lakes and ponds].

### 👉 解析

❶ 中括弧框起來的 which 關係子句是要修飾 a tight "skin"，小括弧框起來的 sometimes called surface tension 也是 a tight "skin"的同位語。這一句開始正式提到本文的主題表面張力，並指出這不是只有小水滴才會有的現象，而是在大面積水域照樣會出現。

❷ tension 是 tense「繃緊的、緊張的」的名詞。加上表示 over 的字首 hyper-（例如 hypertrophy 營養過剩、hypersecretion 分泌過多）成為 hypertension，血管過度繃緊，所以是「高血壓」；反之，加上表示 under 的字首 hypo-（例如 hypotrophy 營養不良、hyposecretion 分泌不足）就成為 hypotension「低血壓」。

# An Uncommon Common Liquid (2)

## 水的平凡與不平凡（2）

💡 閱讀原文：試用 3 分鐘的時間念完文章，記得先
把中文遮上，並翻頁看題目問什麼。計時開始！

### An Uncommon Common Liquid (2)

While surface tension serves the spider well, it can pose a problem for you. (A) When doing the laundry, you might think water gets your clothes wet—and it does. In fact, water doesn't get them nearly as wet as it might. As just mentioned, water molecules prefer their own company so they tend to stick together. (B) As a result of surface tension, water does not readily enter the tiny **recesses** found in the **fibers** of fabrics. To make water wash better, you cannot but reduce its surface tension so it wets things more **uniformly**. (C) **Surfactants** do another important job too. One end of their molecule is attracted to water, while the other end to dirt or **grease**. (D) Therefore, the surfactant molecules help water to get a hold of dirt or grease, break it up, and wash it away – This property is known as **hydrophobic**, meaning "water fearing."

## 水的平凡與不平凡（2）

　　表面張力讓小蜘蛛輕功水上漂，但是卻會給你帶來一個問題。(A) 洗衣時，你可能認為水把衣服浸濕了，沒錯都濕了。事實上，並沒有濕透。如同上述，水分子喜歡結黨成群，因此常常緊緊相擁。(B) 因為表面張力的緣故，水很難鑽進紡織纖維上的細微凹處。為了讓水洗濯效果更好，就不得不降低表面張力，以便讓水可以更均勻的把衣服浸濕。(C) 表面活性劑還有另一個功用。它們的分子其中一端會吸住水，而另一端則是吸住灰塵或油脂。(D) 因此表面活性劑的分子有助於水把灰塵或油脂抓住、分解、洗掉——這種特性就是為世人所知的疏水性，意思是「怕水」。

Look at the four letters that indicate where the following sentence could be added to the passage.

**Since water alone can't clean clothes, try adding some detergents, the surfactants in which improve water's ability to wet things, spread over surfaces, and penetrate into the tight spaces between the threads in your clothes.**

Where could the sentence best fit?

看看文章裡四個字母，哪個地方可以把下面句子安插進去

既然單靠水無法把衣服洗乾淨，那就試試這一招，加點清潔劑。清潔劑裡頭的表面活性劑可以提升水的浸泡能力，在表面上擴散出去，滲進衣服纖維中的緊密空間裡。

這句子放哪裡最合適？

解析

答案｜(C)

❶ 插入句題型要碰到代名詞、指示詞，機率很低，很多場合還是要自求多福，逐字把題目句仔細看清楚，從中抽絲剝繭找出蛛絲馬跡，或多或少總是可以理出一點頭緒。從一開頭 Since water alone can't clean clothes…，可以判斷出題目

句之前應該是表面張力這個特性會讓衣服不容易洗乾淨。接下來又提到…try adding some detergents…解決方案來了，重要的是也提到一個重要名詞 surfactant，就是這玩意可以把衣服洗乾淨。從這可以判斷出題目句之後應該還會繼續提到 detergent、surfactant。

❷ (A) 選項之前只提到 a problem，而 a problem 到底是什麼還是問號。重要的是，衣服不容易洗乾淨的內容還沒提到，所以 (A) 不對。

❸ (B) 選項以前的句子總算開始露出端倪了，這兩句話是解釋害衣服不容易洗乾淨的元凶竟然是表面張力，可是感覺話似乎還沒講完，因為往下又繼續解釋這種情況。

❹ 緊接 (C) 選項後面第一個字就是 surfactant，正好跟題目句呼應。核對上下文邏輯確定 (C) 就是正確答案。

## ⚙ 深度應用分析：對付閱讀就是要化「繁」為「簡」。先刪去( )、[ ]內的文字，找出主要的主詞和動詞！

❶ Since water alone can't clean clothes, try adding some detergents, [the surfactants in which improve water's

從拆解科學、科技類題目，看不定詞、動名詞的角色

ability to (wet things), (spread over surfaces), and (penetrate into the tight spaces between the threads in your clothes).]

## 解析

❶ 中括弧框起來的關係子句修飾 detergents。小括弧框起來的是表示表面活性劑可以提升水的滲透能力

❷ 英文有些動詞後面可以接不定詞，也可以接動名詞，但是語意不同，例如 remember、forget、stop、regret、go on 等，try 也是其中之一。try 後面接動名詞時，是指嘗試去做做看，看看這一招管不管用；接不定詞時，應該視為表目的的(in order) to，亦即為了達成某個目的所以想辦法去做。例如：

* I tried pushing the door, but I found it locked.（我試著去推門，卻發現它上鎖了。）推門只是一種手段。假如沒效，或許還可以試試找鑰匙、爬窗戶……。
* He tried to talk to his boss about a raise but in vain.（為了跟老闆談加薪的事，他嘗試過但無效。）目的就是要老闆談一下。

題目句的 try 後面接動名詞是建議讀者加點清潔劑這個招數，看看靈不靈。假如不靈，還可以再試試用溫水洗、翻滾沖洗……。

❷ (One end of their molecule is attracted to water), while (the other end to dirt or grease).

👉 **解析**

❶ while 連接兩個句子，解釋表面活性劑的分子有兩端，一端水吸住水，另一端吸住灰塵、油脂。

❷ 後面那句話 the other end 後面原本是有 is attracted，但是因為跟前面那句話一模一樣，所以省略掉，只留下介系詞 to。

❸ 從形音義不難求出 attract、train、truck 三者的交集，答案是 drag、draw，也就是都有一股抽、拖、拉的力量。知道這一點，為什麼 trawl 是「拖網」，甚至 tow 是「拖」，都能舉一反三了。這個拖拉家族有衍生出自己特有的字根 tract，例如：
extract= ex(out) + tract「萃取、摘要」就是把精華抽取出來
abstract= abs(away、off) + tract「抽象」就是把意象從客體中抽離出來；subtract= sub(under) + tract「扣除、減去」字根結構有釜底抽薪的感覺；distract = dis(away) + tract。把人家的心拉走，所以是「使……分心」。

# The Most Important Chemical Reaction in the World (1)

## 世界上最重要的化學反應（1）

💡 閱讀原文：試用 3 分鐘的時間念完文章，記得先把中文遮上，並翻頁看題目問什麼。計時開始！

**The Most Important Chemical Reaction in the World (1)**

Almost all life on earth is powered by energy imparted by the sun. Living things that make their own food, such as plants, algae, and some bacteria, are called autotrophs. These autotrophs capture energy from the sun and use it directly or store it for future use, while other organisms, called heterotrophs, eat autotrophs and extract the energy and nutrients stored in their cells. Thus, directly or indirectly, the energy that powers almost all life is derived from the sun. But what allows plants to change sunlight into the stuff of life?

Within the cells of plants are chemicals that cause reactions to take place. In this case, the key chemical is chlorophyll, the green-colored **pigment** capable of trapping blue and red light, which is critical to photosynthesis, the most important chemical reaction in the living world, so to speak. During this seemingly simple reaction, solar energy and chlorophyll cause the carbon dioxide and water in the atmosphere to combine and form sugar and oxygen.

## 世界上最重要的化學反應（1）

　　幾乎地球所有生命都由太陽給予的能量所驅動。像植物、藻類、某些細菌之類可以自行生產食物的生物叫做自營生物。這些自營生物從太陽捕捉能源，直接使用或儲存以備不時之需；其他生物叫做異營生物，異營生物吃自營生物，汲取它們儲存在細胞裡的能量與養分。因此驅動幾乎所有生命的能量直接或間接都源自太陽。然而是什麼因素讓植物可以把陽光轉換成生命的物質呢？

　　在植物的細胞裡有可以引發反應的化學物質。在這種情況下，那個關鍵化學物質就是葉綠素，這是可以捕捉藍光、紅光的綠色色素，它對光合作用至關緊要，而光合作用又可以說是世界上最重要的化學反應。在這乍看之下似乎很簡單的反應中，太陽能和葉綠素讓大氣中的二氧化碳和水結合，產生糖分和水分。

**The author uses the phrase "so to speak" in the last paragraph in order to**

(A) indicate a change in subject from chlorophyll to photosynthesis.

(B) express disagreement that chlorophyll is not so important to photosynthesis.

(C) explain why photosynthesis is the most important chemical reaction in the living world.

(D) call the reader's attention to the significance of photosynthesis.

作者最後一段裡面用 so to speak 這個片語，目的是要

(A) 表示話題從葉綠素轉移到光合作用。

(B) 不贊成葉綠素對光合作用很重要的這個說法。

(C) 解釋何以光合作用是世界上最重要的化學反應。

(D) 讓讀者注意到光合作用的重要。

### 解析

答案｜(D)

❶ 用到 so to speak「可以說是」這個詞，即使不像字面上那麼誇張，但是雖不中亦不遠矣，因此這種修飾用法作用應該

是，透過強調讓讀者注意到作者想表達的想法，所以答案就是 (D)。

❷ chlorophyll 讓很多人一看就想打退堂鼓。chlorophyll 後面字根 phyll「葉」比較不食人間煙火，相關字彙往往躲在科研象牙塔裡，例如 xanthophyll「葉黃素類」、phyllophagous「吃樹葉的」；前面字根 chloro 就比較常常飛入尋常百姓家，像英文女孩名字 Chloe 應該很耳熟吧！Chloe 就是來自「黃綠色」的單字家族，其他還有：

chlorine「氯」的顏色是黃綠色，化學元素符號 Cl 就是這個字；

choler「膽汁」。膽汁是金黃色，但是濃縮後是綠色。膽汁滯留會引發黃疸症狀，糞便是黃褐色也是因為膽汁的緣故；

cholera「霍亂」會嚴重上吐下瀉，連膽汁都吐出來，古人便誤以為這種傳染病是膽汁失調所造成；

melancholy = melan(black) + choly。根據古希臘名醫希波克拉提斯的體液理論，黑膽汁分泌過多會導致「憂鬱」。

從拆解科學、科技類題目，看不定詞、動名詞的角色

## 深度應用分析：對付閱讀就是要化「繁」為「簡」。先刪去( )、[ ] 內的文字，找出主要的主詞和動詞！

**❶** In this case, the key chemical is chlorophyll, (the green-colored pigment capable of trapping blue and red light), [which is critical to photosynthesis, (the most important chemical reaction in the living world, so to speak)].

### ☞ 解析

**❶** 第一個小括弧框起來的 the green-colored pigment capable of trapping blue and red light 是 chlorophyll 的同位語，亦即說明葉綠素是什麼東西；第二個小括弧框起來的 the most important chemical reaction in the living world, so to speak 是 photosynthesis 的同位語，亦即強調光合作用的重要性。中括弧框起來的關係子句 which is critical⋯是要修飾 chlorophyll，說明葉綠素乃光合作用不可或缺。

**❷** so to speak 是獨立不定詞，意思是「可以說是」，例如：
The new procedures have been officially put into practice, so to speak.
（新措施可以說已經正式實施了。）
Orchid Island is a lone island off the coast of Taiwan, a

mere dot, so to speak, in the Bashi Channel.

（蘭嶼是台灣外海的一座小島，可以說是巴士海峽上的一個小點。）

❸ 獨立不定詞一般都要用逗號跟句中其他部分隔開，做副詞修飾整句。重要的獨立不定詞還有 to begin with「首先」、to be sure「的確」、to do one justice「公平而論」、to get back to the point「言歸正傳」、to put it another way「換句話說」。

❷ [These autotrophs capture energy from the sun and use it directly or store it for future use]; while [other organisms, (called heterotrophs), eat autotrophs and extract the energy and nutrients(stored in their cells)].

### 解析

❶ while 連接兩個用中括弧框起來的對比句子，比較自營生物和異營生物的差異。

❷ 第一個小括弧框起來的分詞片語 called heterotrophs 修飾 other organisms；第二個小括弧框起來的分詞片語 stored in their cells 修飾 the energy and nutrients。

# The Most Important Chemical Reaction in the World (2)

世界上最重要的化學反應（2）

閱讀原文：試用 3 分鐘的時間念完文章，記得先
把中文遮上，並翻頁看題目問什麼。計時開始！

**The Most Important Chemical Reaction in the World (2)**

But the reaction is not really as simple as it seems, for there are a number of steps. First a series of steps called the light reactions bind the energy of light into molecules that are later used to build sugar molecules. (A) The solar energy is absorbed by chlorophyll and converted into chemical energy stored in the **bonds** of an **intermediate** compound. During this phase, water is **decomposed**, **ultimately** giving off oxygen and leaving hydrogen **ions** behind. This oxygen is then **accessible** to you and other living things. (B)

Other steps in this process of photosynthesis do not require light energy and are therefore called the dark reactions. (C) This simple sugar and the atoms they contain are the building blocks from which almost all other living tissue is built. (D) Photosynthesis generates all the breathable oxygen in the atmosphere and renders plants rich in nutrients. For scientists, this is a topic well worth researching.

## 世界上最重要的化學反應（2）

　　但是這個反應其實沒有表面上那麼簡單，因為它有好幾個步驟。首先叫做光反應的那一系列步驟把光能量結合成分子，這些分子以後可以用來製造糖分子。(A) 太楊能被葉綠素吸收並轉換成化學能源，儲存在中間化合物的化學鍵裡。在這階段，水分被分解掉，最後釋放出氧氣，留下氫離子。之後你和其他生物就可以呼吸到這氧氣了。(B)

　　光合作用過程中其他步驟並不需要光能量，因此叫做暗（碳）反應。(C) 單醣和它們所含的原子就是構成所有其他生命組織的基本原件。(D) 光合作用產生大氣中所有可供呼吸的氧氣，還並且讓植物富含養分──對科學家來説，這實在是非常值得研究的一個主題。

Look at the four letters that indicate where the following sentence could be added to the passage.

**During this stage the energy from the intermediate chemical, the hydrogen ions, and carbon dioxide combine into simple sugar, some of which is used to provide energy for the growth and development of plants while the rest is stored in leaves, roots, or fruits for later use by plants.**

Where could the sentence best fit?

看看文章裡四個字母，哪個地方可以把下面句子安插進去

在這階段中，中間化合物的能量、氫離子、二氧化碳結合成單醣，其中一些單醣被用來提供植物生長發育所需的能量，其餘則是被植物儲存在樹葉、根部、果實留待日後使用。

這句子放哪裡最合適？

👉 解析

答案｜(C)

❶ 題目句的指示詞 this 證明之前一定提到某個過程，而這句話打蛇隨棍上，解釋這個過程會產生單醣以及植物會如何處理這些單醣。

❷ 把文章從頭看下來，可以發現 (A) 選項不盡理想，因為 (A) 之前那句話說 First a series of steps called the light reactions bind the energy of light…後面幾接著又說 The solar energy is absorbed…，前後都提到『陽光』，可是題目句卻隻字不提，這證明這兩句是一脈相承。

❸ 同理，(B) 選項也大有問題，因為題目句幾乎以 simple sugar 為核心，可是 (B) 之前的句子卻連個 sugar 影子都沒看到。放到這種位置當然很突兀。

❹ 只要認真看一眼，就可以感覺，沒錯，(C) 應該是正確答案的不二選擇了，因為前面…called the dark reactions 正好提到一個過程；後面緊接的句子劈頭就是 This simple sugar and the atoms they contain…也跟題目句核心吻合。這麼完美的答案還真是打著燈籠都找不到。

❺ 假如答案不是 (C)，而是 (D)，那麼原先 (C) 這個位置顯然會出現一個 missing link，所以只能跟 (D) 說聲抱歉。

從拆解科學、科技類題目，看不定詞、動名詞的角色

## ⚙️ 深度應用分析：對付閱讀就是要化「繁」為「簡」。先刪去( )、[ ] 內的文字，找出主要的主詞和動詞！

❶ During this stage the energy from the intermediate chemical, the hydrogen ions, and carbon dioxide combine into simple sugar, [(some of which is used to provide energy for the growth and development of plants) while (the rest is stored in leaves, roots, or fruits for later use by plants)].

### 👉 解析

❶ 中括弧框起來的關係子句 some of which…for later use by plants 修飾先行詞 simple sugar，解釋光合作用的暗反應產生的單醣做何用途。

❷ 關係子句裡面還有一個連接詞 while 連接兩個小括弧框起來的子句，說明部分單醣被植物用來發育成長，部分則是儲存起來。

❸ 本句的 be used to 後面接原形動詞，是很單純的 use 被動用法，不要把這種用法跟另外兩個跟 use 有關的用法混淆：一種是 used to 接動詞原形，注意沒有 be 動詞，表示過去的習慣，例如：I weigh less than I used to.（我的體重比以前

輕了。）；另一種是 be used to 接動名詞，意思是『習慣』，這個 to 是介系詞。凡是 to 當介系詞使用的場合都很重要，因為很容易誤以為是不定詞。例如：He is used to eating in this restaurant.（他習慣在這家餐廳吃飯。）、I'm not used to the extreme heat.（我不習慣這種酷熱。）

❷ For scientists, this is a topic well worth researching.

### 👉 解析

❶ 雖然 worthy 跟 worth 只差一個字母，但是用法卻截然不同

可以說         **a worthy book**      （一本有價值的書）

但是卻不能說   **a worth book**

可以說         **Education is worthy.**（教育是很值得的）

但是卻不能說   **Education is worth.**

worthy 後面要先來個介系詞 of，而後再接名詞、代名詞；假如接動詞的話，既可以寫成不定詞，也可以放在 of 後面，改成動名詞。不管是寫成不定詞，還是動名詞，都必須呈現『被動』的形式，完全跟 worth 天差地別。例如：

The movie is worth seeing.= The movie is worthy of being seen.= The movie is worthy to be seen.= The movie is worth your while to see.= It is worth (your) while to see the movie. = It pays to see the movie.

（這部電影值得一看。）

# ─職場英語─

一本專為航空地勤量身打造【職前準備+在職進修】的必備職場英語工具書！Upgrade工作英語能力 & 職場EQ！

書　系：Learn Smart 056
書　名：Ground Crew English航空地勤的每一天（MP3）
定　價：NT$ 380元
ISBN：978-986-91915-9-3
規　格：平裝/320頁/17x23cm/雙色印刷/附光碟

最基礎、最易學的餐飲口說英語！讓餐飲從業人員、餐飲科系師生、外商餐飲業的社會人士，都讚聲連連的英語工具書！

書　系：Leader 044
書　名：Easy & Basic餐飲口說英語(附MP3)
定　價：NT$ 380元
ISBN： 978-986-92856-3-6
規　格：平裝/304頁/17x23cm/雙色印刷/附光碟

最具指標性的空服員英語應試手冊，100%符合航空公司與個人特質的面試應答！擺脫一成不變的準備方式，加深考官印象，更替自己加分！

書　系：Learn Smart 059
書　名：王牌空服員100% 應試秘笈（附MP3）
定　價：NT$ 379元
ISBN：978-986-92855-2-0
規　格：平裝/288頁/17x23cm/雙色印刷/附光碟

最時尚、最「身歷其境感」的精華英語對答！秘書特助、行銷、公關，想要脫穎而出，不僅要加倍努力，還需要為你的職場英文實力加分！

書　系：Leader 049
書　名：時尚秘書英語 （附MP3）
定　價：NT$ 380元
ISBN：978-986-92856-8-1
規　格：平裝/304頁/17x23cm/雙色印刷/附光碟

用故事區分，以及介系詞的"功能概念"分類，搭配圖解例句，考試不再和關鍵分數擦身而過，也是閱讀、寫作與口說的必備用書！

書　系：Leader 048
書　名：圖解介系詞、看故事學片語：第一本文法魔法書
定　價：NT\$ 360元
ISBN：978-986-92856-7-4
規　格：平裝/320頁/17x23cm/雙色印刷

獨家吵架英語秘笈大公開！精選日常生活情境＋道地慣用語，教你適時地表達看法爭取應得的權利，成為最有文化的英語吵架王！

書　系：Learn Smart 064
書　名：冤家英語（MP3）
定　價：NT\$ 360元
ISBN：978-986-92855-6-8
規　格：平裝/304頁/17x23cm/雙色印刷/附光碟

享受異國風光，走訪知名美食熱點；帶著情感品嚐美食，才是人間美味；用英語表達富情感意涵的美食，才算得上是『食尚』。

書　系：Leader 050
書　名：餐飲英語：異國美食情緣(MP3)
定　價：NT\$ 369元
ISBN：978-986-92856-9-8
規　格：平裝/288頁/17x23cm/雙色印刷/附光碟

**Learn Smart! 072**

## iBT 新托福閱讀：解構式學習，化繁為「剪」

| | |
|---|---|
| 作　　　者 | 王盟雄 |
| 發 行 人 | 周瑞德 |
| 執行總監 | 齊心瑀 |
| 行銷經理 | 楊景輝 |
| 企劃編輯 | 饒美君 |
| 封面構成 | 高鍾琪 |

| | |
|---|---|
| 內頁構成 | 菩薩蠻數位文化有限公司 |
| 印　　製 | 大亞彩色印刷製版股份有限公司 |
| 初　　版 | 2017 年 1 月 |
| 定　　價 | 新台幣 380 元 |
| 出　　版 | 倍斯特出版事業有限公司 |
| 電　　話 | (02) 2351-2007 |
| 傳　　真 | (02) 2351-0887 |
| 地　　址 | 100 台北市中正區福州街 1 號 10 樓之 2 |
| E - m a i l | best.books.service@gmail.com |
| 網　　址 | www.bestbookstw.com |

| | |
|---|---|
| 港澳地區總經銷 | 泛華發行代理有限公司 |
| 地　　　　址 | 香港新界將軍澳工業邨駿昌街 7 號 2 樓 |
| 電　　　　話 | (852) 2798-2323 |
| 傳　　　　真 | (852) 2796-5471 |

### 國家圖書館出版品預行編目資料

iBT 新托福閱讀：解構式學習,化繁為「剪」/
王盟雄著. -- 初版. -- 臺北市：倍斯特,
2017.01 面；公分. -- (Learn Smart!；72)
ISBN 978-986-93766-5-5 (平裝)
1.托福考試

　　805.1894　　　　　　　105023414